First Comes
Summer

First Comes Summer

MARIA HESSELAGER

Translated by Martin Aitken

RIVERHEAD BOOKS

NEW YORK · 2023

RIVERHEAD BOOKS
An imprint of Penguin Random House LLC
penguinrandomhouse.com

Copyright © 2021 by Maria Hesselager
English translation copyright © 2023 by Martin Aitken

First published in Denmark as *Jeg hedder Folkví* by Gutkind Forlag, Copenhagen, in 2021
First English-language edition published by Riverhead, 2023

LIBRARY OF CONGRESS CATALOGING-IN-PUBLICATION DATA
Names: Hesselager, Maria, author. | Aitken, Martin, translator.
Title: First comes summer / Maria Hesselager ; translated by Martin Aitken.
Other titles: Jeg hedder Folkví. English
Description: First English-language edition. |
New York : Riverhead Books, 2023.
Identifiers: LCCN 2022030898 (print) | LCCN 2022030899 (ebook) |
ISBN 9780593542606 (hardcover) | ISBN 9780593542620 (ebook)
Subjects: LCGFT: Psychological fiction. | Novels.
Classification: LCC PT8177.18.E86 J4413 2023 (print) |
LCC PT8177.18.E86 (ebook) | DDC 839.813/8—dc23/eng/20220725
LC record available at https://lccn.loc.gov/2022030898
LC ebook record available at https://lccn.loc.gov/2022030899

Printed in the United States of America
1st Printing

BOOK DESIGN BY LUCIA BERNARD

There was a girl, her name was Folkvi
She lived in a different age
She spent her life at Frøsted

In wintertime the sky was white
It was white, almost mild
No, no, it was cruel

But what does it matter
When first comes summer

First Comes
Summer

The sun has not yet risen. It will be the warmest day of the harvest month. From the house Folkví comes carrying her brother's bride, Gerd. She crosses the headman's open yard and cuts through a scattering of pine trees, then with her hip shoves open the door of a small wooden shed.

Four torches illuminate the dark walls. A simple table, a wooden figurine, and the light that spills in from the door. Folkví puts Gerd down on the table and smooths the girl's hair away from her face, then winds it tightly about her hand. She locks an arm around Gerd's head and presses an elbow down on her throat. Gerd's mouth goes taut, her eyes widen as Folkví tries to part her lips with the cup, she kicks at the air. Folkví grips Gerd's hair tighter and presses harder against her windpipe until the face in front of her contorts, then after a moment its muscles slacken. When again she tries to force the henbane between Gerd's lips, the girl no longer resists. The cloudy brown liquid dribbles from the corners of her mouth to run together at the chin and drip onto the white sark, stains seeping into the fabric. Folkví releases her and goes outside to fetch a handcart. The air is still. It's getting light.

The Book
of Folkví

The Summer of the Offering

The evening sky is gray, overcast, and Od stands with his hands together in front of his crotch, legs slightly apart, head lowered, until the door is opened. He raises his head then and beams a smile, as the light from inside spills orange upon him. Folkví is a dim silhouette. Her eyes are swollen, her voice hoarse, No, is all she says when she sees him, and slams the door shut. He stares into the rough timber, shakes his head, unsure of himself, senses a warmth in his cheeks. All the way through the woods he's been toying with little anecdotes to tell her, he's imagined the two of them by the fire, drinking. And then she receives him like this. Or rather, doesn't receive him at all. Now the whole evening's awry. And how familiar, he thinks, how familiar, that joy should turn to disappointment. He's only twenty-one, and it's not so much that he finds her attractive, although he does—sometimes he'll catch himself just watching her while she talks to someone, say, or stands outside in the chill of morning, which makes her skin so radiant: fresh, she is then, like a wind, and strong. He adores watching her, even in her awkwardness, the way her slender trunk curves into her hips, the childlike gusto in her gait. Only a couple of nights before, they knocked about restlessly, and as morning approached, she jumped in the fjord while he sat and watched from the shore. Her fair skin shimmered in the blue darkness as she came up out of the water, she came naked toward him with her broad hips and halted in front of him, dripping and smiling, and wrung her long hair down on him, dousing his face. She lay down in the grass, and with their faces turned toward each other they talked until day. In the light in which he sees her when he thinks of it—in that light she is exhilarating. Naked and almost unbelievable. And yet it's not the way she looks, there's something else about her, a determination, as if she is driven by some private purpose, he's not sure. She's the one, always, who determines the direction of their discussions, the moods that prevail between them, it makes her seem completely alien to him. In this way he becomes somewhat alien to himself. He does things that only a few months ago, before he knew her, he would not have comprehended, things that would have made him think, *No one can be worth such humiliation.* Like now, for instance, as he raises his hand and knocks on her door again. Without response. He shouts her name, and then again, and at this she appears once more, though she scarcely looks at him, only places her hands flat against his chest to push him away: What is it you don't understand, Od, she says. Go home. He sees her swollen face and wishes only to stay, yet he pulls up his hood and turns to leave. And Folkví closes the door behind him and feels distraught at the injustice of fate, that now he must wander home, disappointed and without release, to this she is not indifferent. Od's visit sparks an irritability in her that she doesn't know what to do with, and now she drinks with even less restraint than before. She thinks about love. How unfair it is. The weird, twining threads of the Norns.

The wind buffets the house in the night, it rushes wildly in the pines. At dawn the rain pours down. Folkví stands outside in it, leaning against the fence that encloses the headman's yard, a hand on the smooth oakwood. She is drunk and distant, removed from herself; she stands in the rain and barely senses it fall. She barely senses the morning light either, yet it lends her a certain mood, a feeling that perhaps everything will be all right, the world is still here. It's hard to think beyond that. She has been offered a lull in her woe. She sits down on one of the big stones in front of the fence and looks across the meadowland in the direction of the village, sees the sky change color as the rain begins to ease. Everything is still, and everything has meaning: her cold feet, the slow shift of sky as the darkness dissolves from below. It is a familiar feeling: now she is sitting here. She trembles from the alcohol, from hunger and cold, but the stone on which she sits is good, and over the pines light seeps through the cover of cloud; it is a gray and yellow morning. Her breathing is shallow. Yesterday is a physical thing that fills her body, it is not a thought. She feels her buttocks against the stone. All that exists now is she herself, the stone and the meadows that came long before her, and also the rising sun. The stone is smooth with rain. How strange it is that time still passes, even though Áslakr has said he is to marry. It is wild and brutal, but the sun, unmoved, still draws its chariot across the sky. Day after day, it is indifferent.

Much can change in a day and a night. She has paced about the house, risen and settled, without sleep; she hasn't had a peaceful moment since Áslakr told her of his coming marriage. Then he went away. While she yelled and begged for him to stay, he went away. Too big for her own skin, that's what she is. It feels strange to shout when you are alone; her despair lost its shape when Áslakr left the house. So she began drinking steadily and intensely, mumbling verse and singing to the gods, but they could not help her here, all she could do was call on them: Look at me, in my miserable hours. A branch batted the house. She called on Freya, who is supposed to soothe all sorrows of the heart, and yet it didn't help, she still feels a pain in her chest. The air resists being drawn into her lungs as she sits in the drizzle. Áslakr's face, the way he gripped her to stop her onslaught, his hands as he spoke, the spirit she'd been in when the evening began, she can't stop flinching when she thinks of it. She narrows her eyes, remembering how she tried to grab him and keep hold of him, how he protested and wrenched away, said, Folkví! I won't. How fine she had made herself too, how excited she'd been to learn what was afoot, for he'd been solemn when he'd asked if she was going to be home that evening, there was something they had to talk about. Now, what's wrong with now, she'd asked, but he'd said no, we need time to talk about it, and inside she lit up, he's broken up with Gerd, she told herself, because he looked at her so directly. It seemed to her that he was staring, and she felt the palms of her hands become warm, a thrust of her loins toward him. The misunderstanding had been complete, and now she covers her face with her hand. She had made herself pretty and knocked back a few drinks with one of the thralls while waiting for him to come, almost singing aloud as she puttered about their childhood home, tidying up to pass the time. She had triumphed over Gerd. The relief in her body, the evening lay ahead of her like a promise. Already drunk when he arrived, she had clasped his face and kissed him almost as soon as he began to speak, for there was no need for such gravity, no cause for worry, he looked so serious. Couldn't he see, it was all going to work out. They would find a way. You open a door and go into a house, now they were opening this one. She held him tightly, a hand around his neck, but he wrenched away, shook his head. No, Folkví. It's not that. I've betrothed myself.

She is cuffed by a gust of wind, and shrinks. Stares at a leaf in front of her feet. It mustn't be true that she is not what he longs for. But there is no more to be lost, and so she gets to her feet. It's as if he isn't thinking straight. He's seen Gerd, what, once, and now she is to be his wife? But he has known Folkví always! And behind her back—she swipes at the air, her fingers stiffly splayed—behind her back he has entered into betrothal.

The wind has picked up, her skirts fall cold and wet about her legs; she halts in front of the hird house and takes a swig from the jar. What we fail to say or do shapes life too, and so she knocks on the door. Her frozen knuckles smart. She shouts his name, Áslakr, dismissing as it comes to her the thought of Od, how she is standing now at Áslakr's door as Od stood at hers the evening before, for Áslakr must not feel the same about her as she feels about Od, must not regard her with the same charitable feelings of guilt. But no one feels the same as another in this world, and that is forever the problem. Then Áslakr comes to the door, she stares at him, his gray-blue eyes gleam in his tanned face. His features, young and strong. Behind his glowing brow she sees his soul. She will wash him and care for him, comb his long hair. She would like to punish him too. Folkví, he mutters, seeming neither surprised nor pleased. I was asleep. He steps away from the door so that she may enter, pulls up a stool that she may sit, it scrapes against the stamped earthen floor. The room is dark. Embers glow in the fireplace, light drops through the smoke hole, though not enough to illuminate the elongated space. He yawns and hands her a blanket. You're soaked, he says, throwing an oblique glance that barely grazes her. She wraps herself in the blanket, only to find herself at a loss for words. Her cold red fingers reach for his; a wind whistles in the chinks. Her face feels wrong. Her features feel weighted, her skin drawn about her mouth, where one day age will express itself in long vertical furrows that will meet at her lips. Her eyes fix on a crack in the table. Well, is all Áslakr says, and lets go of her hand, yawning again. I can't really say any more than I said yesterday.

A bit later she lies down on the sleeping berth. Eventually, he comes over and lies down behind her, folds his arm around her waist, his strong arm with its fair hairs. Her hand takes hold of it, on the wide plank bed next to the fire. She feels his breath against her neck and relaxes then in the darkness. Áslakr will look after her. Behind her eyelids the world turns, but now at last she can sleep. Because he is there beside her, she can rest. There is the smell of him and the hide and the cold floor, and the sound of the trees and the rain outside. And while her eyes are closed, the sounds and smells melt together, they tell her all is well at this moment, that she can abandon herself to fatigue and find some peace, as if she were a child.

When she wakes she lies still and looks about. Her eyes blink. It must be well into morning. The door is open, the sky yet gray, though lighter now. The space behind her is empty, Áslakr has risen, perhaps some time ago. Her heart thumps in her chest. Where has he gone? A tear runs from the corner of her left eye to the base of her nose, then gently crosses its bridge to trickle down her cheek, following its folds until it is halted by her hair.

My Name Is Folkvi

At fifteen years old she stood in the feast hall of the headman's house, oddly alone in her new grown-up body, when her father came up and kissed her on the cheek. He tried to say something wise and exhortative to her, but she couldn't understand the slur of his speech in the din and simply nodded and smiled, watching with a feeling of insecurity as her parents left the solstice celebration. Part of her wanted to forge a way through the throng and run after them, to catch up with them a few strides outside the longhouse and tell them, a little breathlessly, that she was tired too and wanted to go home with them. The evening had been full of excitement, overwhelming: to lose yourself in the dance, feeling the strength of the collective energy, the way it makes you forget yourself . . . the energy that can arise between people, reducing them to their common purpose. Then you are only the chain, the changing partners, the repetitions, the set sequence of the steps: you release the women's hands and step forward to the man opposite; the introductory ritual, the curtsy, first left, then right. The stamp of heels, the hands that grip the waist, the brows that touch, the twirling movements across the floor. The smell, the hypnotic backdrop of stringed instruments, the tramping feet and whooping cries, the room rushing by in a dizzying whirl. You lean back, held in your partner's grasp, turn with him upon an invisible axis, keen and concentrated, free. Then you return to female hands, to the circle's edge, palms sweatier than before, to one another's flushed faces, slower steps, until once more it snatches you up: a new partner, a more sinewy frame that takes you with just as firm a lead.

By turns, you immerse yourself in the dance, becoming one with the revelry, and then become aware of the others, the eyes that are upon you, all the little signs people exchange that are the energy not of the celebration but of people and their hierarchies. Who joins the conversation and who leaves? Who is met with nods, laughing acknowledgment, and interested smiles when they speak, and who must struggle, increasingly shrill, to get in a word, to put a viewpoint across, who must expect always to be met with skepticism, to be interrupted and ignored?

Folkví had noticed a young man she'd never seen before, who looked as if he didn't know anyone at the celebration, or at least no one who would pay him any heed. He was perhaps a year or two older than her, sixteen or seventeen, and his sleeves were pulled so far down over his hands it was as if he wished to hide himself completely. His tunic too was of an unusual cut, covering much of his throat, and he'd been squirming there in the dim light against the wall, clutching between his hands one of the chased silver cups belonging to the headman's house. He was looking into the cup constantly, Folkví saw, turning it in his hands, as if to screen out the teeming crowd. He looked so forlorn at simply being visible, caught between the chain dance on one side and the fully occupied long-table on the other, alone in a crowd of outgoing people, though it wasn't his solitariness that touched Folkví so much as the sense that his very presence revealed a wish to be, like everyone else, a part of the revelry, part of the community that apparently frightened the wits out of him and only confirmed the feeling that radiated from him: that the more he wished to transgress his solitariness, the more it grew. She could hardly bear to think how he must have stood at home—or wherever he had come from, the market perhaps—and looked down at himself, reluctantly and yet with some vanity, disdainfully and at the same time with expectancy, for otherwise a person surely wouldn't bother, wouldn't make the effort to go out at all, if they didn't harbor some measure of restlessness, some meager hope that persisted in the thought that they might miss something if they stayed at home. Maybe I'll meet a nice girl, or maybe, if someone says this or that, I'll say this or that in reply, and everyone will smile. Or, at the very least, I'll fall into conversation with someone and I'll be able to tell them then about the last few days, how I managed to haul all those fish out of the sea.

Folkví sat at a long-table and studied him from afar. His features were square and attractive, he was dark-haired, and although she couldn't see his legs properly, she knew his knees touched as he stood. She'd been unsettled by his presence and wanted to go over and talk to him, only she didn't know how. Couldn't manage it, and left him standing there. But then he glanced at her, perhaps sensing her looking at him, perhaps feeling her gaze to be scornful, though it was quite the opposite she wanted, not to scorn but to support him. His eyes found a point behind her where they could rest, as if to suggest that his gaze had merely wandered about the room and brushed her by chance. Still, he'd looked at her, she'd looked at him, their eyes had made contact, and he hadn't smiled, she neither, and now it was too late. Or perhaps not yet too late, but it would have to be right now if she was to go over and stand beside him, her eyes turned to the dancing, and say, Hello, my name is Folkví. The moment was now. It had to be now, if it was to be at all. Folkví's pulse raced, she felt her body tremble. What was the worst that could happen? From where she sat at the table—with no idea what the people around her were talking about, just smiling every now and then when someone laughed—she watched as he put the cup to his mouth. He turned it in his hands again, frothing the last of the ale to knock it back in one gulp, then without looking at Folkví began to move away, following the line of the wall behind the long-tables. Something sank inside her. She smiled an apology at the people she was seated with before rising from the bench and trying to catch up with him, but there were too many people between them, the room was too dark, and he melted into the throng. She pushed her way between the rows of benches, but he was gone. Probably he wanted some fresh air, or perhaps he'd decided to go home, because by the time she got to the door he was nowhere to be seen. Breathless and feeling a stranger to herself, she stood outside the headman's hall and looked up into the open sky. Ai, too bad.

This, along with hundreds of other impressions, not least the realization that men were beginning to address her differently, look at her differently, but also that she herself had begun to react differently to them—now, when she felt someone looking at her, she could return his gaze so intensely and without shame that he would be forced to look away, and she felt a quiet glee in such a game. She put a sway in her hips, and how easy it was! It worked, and it was easy. She would pick out a victim and then stride along the rows of tables where revelers sang and raised their cups to one another or sat deep in conversation, and she could pick out a man, or for that matter a woman, and with her eyes fixed on whoever it was move closer and closer to them, lowering her head a tad but holding the person in her gaze, see how she could prompt them to drop out of their conversations and follow her with their eyes or concentrate on looking nonchalant, and then when she was only a few feet away, she'd drop her gaze and walk on past.

So the evening was long, and eventually she lost interest in the festivities and wanted to go home to the house of her parents, where time stood still. For a moment she was lost, a little drunk in fact, but then it was that Áslakr came over and whispered something in her ear, and then it was that she began to laugh. Only a sliver of air between their bodies. He leaned into her, his brow resting against her head, a hand curled around her waist. A thrill ran through her, a desire to roar out across the headman's hall, but she didn't move, she was almost paralyzed.

The next day they hardly saw each other. Áslakr was practicing with their father, Folkví was clearing up, sweeping and washing, the tips of her fingers wrinkled and pink, she smiled a private smile and gave her head a little shake as she bent over the tub. As evening approached she rolled down her sleeves and went to sit outside in the tall grass against the wall, absently picking at the blades. A wish she couldn't make disappear: that he should lay his hand on her bare abdomen. The sun was low and red, the air cool, and the soil too cooled after a time. Áslakr's gaze when he watched her, so clear in its intent, she felt it now, what before had been hidden, though no less real, was unmistakable now. That was how it felt. She looked up, and over the crest of the hill just then came Áslakr's hair, then his forehead, then his whole body, walking along the path to their house with his characteristic gait, a softness about his knees. His fair hair falling into his face. He lifted a hand a little in greeting, then fixed his eyes on the ground in front of him again.

Hello, Áslakr, she said in a hoarse voice once he was within earshot. Sit down here with me. She was enlivened by his arrival, words streamed from her mouth. She talked about everything but the celebration. She asked him how he was. Like a child she leaned her head against his shoulder, placed her hands against his chest, crouched before him, and grasped his hand to explore it as she babbled on. First the palm with all its lines, tracing them with her forefinger, then the back of the hand, his grubby fingernails. Each time he spoke she wanted to interrupt, she wanted to laugh. Who are you in love with, Áslakr? she asked, holding his hand between hers, cleaning under the nails. I know, it's Aud, isn't it? He looked at her. There's no one, he said after a pause. I'm not in love with anyone. He smiled and withdrew his hand, and she laid her head in his lap. She looked out across the yard, where people stood chatting two by two or went about their errands, a horse was drawn into the stable. It was a mild evening, the earth was cold. Her body felt big. And all the time there was the cry that sat in her chest, a roar of some kind, this rattle, this tickle beneath her ribs that she could not be rid of. She wanted to shout out with all her might. She wanted to knock him to the ground with a shove against his shoulders, to fell him and pin him down. But she remained with her head in his lap, watching the gloaming sky as Áslakr absently ran his hand through her hair, his calm voice speaking to her. That day he had been better with the bow than ever before. It was a strange feeling.

★

When she was little, someone had to look after her. She crept to her mother in the night, snuggling into a ball, wanting to be smaller even than that, to lie with her face buried in an armpit. Her mother was animal. The soft skin of her mother's tummy, on which she warmed her little hands, her drowsy, listless movements. Don't do that, Folkví, I don't like it. And then Folkví would fold her short arms around her mother's waist, under blankets smelling of wool and the inscrutable female sex, a carnal smell reminiscent of the stables. Here she could sleep, always. Her mother must never go away. In the long nights, Folkví's thoughts could drift between memories, notions, and dreams, the great giants of Utgard might clutch at her ankles, but then she would turn over onto her other side, sensing the body that lay beside her, and again her thoughts would wander in some new direction, pulling her with them. When the light came in the mornings, Folkví wished only to keep her eyes shut, she was a closed room, an extension of her mother. A hand rested against the back of her head. She would never again enjoy so simple a relationship with anyone, the big white thighs shifting under the blankets, the light and the smell, the gentle touch that said, sleep on.

The Summer of the Offering

The thralls are afraid, Od sees, they don't want to enter Folkví's house, they're scared of the evil spirits. He doesn't chastise them but allows them to leave as soon as they've brought in the food. He sweeps the floors himself. In the mornings, he leaves the door open so the spirits are free to go out, but he will not depart from her. When he returned, the day after Folkví slammed the door in his face, he found her in a corner of the house, cowering, an arm raised to shield herself from the light he let in—like a pigeon, he thought, like an injured pigeon, trapped indoors, a wing held aloft in a final appeal: Don't take me, but if you do, let me not see it—and he caved in then, forgot everything he'd prepared to say (for example: You haven't the right to treat me like that. I may be of a different standing than you, and you may think I ought to be grateful for your attentions, but I'm still a free man, and I don't know what you become when you behave as if you don't want to know me, as if I were an enemy. And also: There's a limit, and that limit is here). Folkví, he said when he saw her there, curled up on the floor, what's the matter with you? He crouched down and stroked her back.

Now he brings in a wooden bowl and sits on the edge of the bed. She has gone all thin and greasy. Her eyes are dull, but her face gleams. He washes her a bit, a wet cloth to her neck, then dipped in the bowl, drawn along the line of her spine, dipped in the bowl, armpits, bowl. You smell like an invalid, he says, but she doesn't reply, simply allows him to turn her onto her back so that he can wash her abdomen.

The pines sway, dragging their branches across the roof. It's the only thing she hears, sounds that swell. Folkví walks her fingers over her stomach, beneath her ribs an abrupt drop, she has grown skinny, her hip bones are sharp. She pulls the blankets up to her nose and turns onto her side, once again allows her eyes to fall shut, a rank smell in her nostrils, of something buttery. Her hair is thick and stiff, matted, and yesterday she rubbed skin from her body, thin flakes of blackish brown she tucked under her pillow. Open, says Od. He puts a spoon into her mouth. Good, Folkví. A little of a lukewarm herbal extract trickles down her throat, most of it already sticky on her chin or seeped into the pillow. Her vision is diminished, her eyes move about the room, but everything beyond Od is a shimmer. She closes her eyes again, seeing now only scintillating darkness, a gleaming, yellowy murk, until sleep grasps her and drags her down. It feels like a fall from her body, the dream deep, shaftlike.

Áslakr's voice mingles with images of a room filled with people. The sound of the door opening to the outside world, footsteps and dissonance, the voices of Áslakr and Od growing louder, and she now has the option of waking. But she turns back, into her dream. Áslakr, sitting on a toppled tree in front of her, telling her about his childhood as if she'd never been a part of it, so eagerly he speaks, and in detail: I had two parents, a sister, I loved the long summers when I would help out in the fields, my muscles were small and hard beneath the skin, and as he talks he becomes a boy before her eyes. He declares his love for her, quite unspectacularly, simply straightens his back and tells her he loves her, with the earnest expression of a child. And she laughs, her mouth open wide, triumphant, she can sense and see herself at the same time. The house in which they stand is infinite, she draws him through new rooms, one after another, runs as she fables about these unfamilar spaces, brimming with a quiet joy.

A gasp and it's all gone, the blanket snatched away, the dream and its good hold with it. The body isn't a problem when you're asleep. Stop it, she breathes, unprotected and cold, stop it. She twists to grab back the cover. Give it to me. In the sheen of daylight she senses Áslakr at the side of the bed, narrows her eyes, draws her legs up as if to scrabble back into her web of dreams. But she's cold. The dream murmurs, rises, and is lost. Next to her instead is Áslakr, too much a man now. He snaps the blanket in the air, shakes it while looking at Od, who stands nearby. Is she eating? he asks, spreading the blanket on top of her. He is here. No, Od replies. Hardly at all. Áslakr adjusts the blanket, swaddles her feet, and looks her in the eye, at last you're awake, he says. She says nothing but pulls the blanket tight and glares at him, her pulse throbbing in her throat, so forcefully that it hurts. He must never go away. Áslakr clears his throat softly. Anyway, says Od. I'll wait outside. Yes, says Áslakr. I'll see you there. Od nods a farewell.

The straw crunches as Áslakr sits down on her bed. Then the familiar smell, his smell of hair and skin, the same as ever. She lifts her head onto his thigh and glances at Od, the shrug of his shoulders, his gently forward-leaning gait. The door creaks as he leaves the house, and she turns to Áslakr, parts her parched lips. Her whole body is drained. Tears run down her cheeks but she makes no sound, she looks into his eyes and says nothing. She wants to cry, because he's her brother, the thought is as dark and as vast as a forest, and she wants him to be struck by it too, by how incredible it is that their lives should be woven together, there's no proper way to express it. It hurts to know something he hasn't grasped. She senses he can't deal with her when she's like this, but he feels obligated. His patience is gone. Folkví? His voice sounds weary, and he clears his throat. You're my sister, nothing can alter that. But I refuse to keep having this conversation. I really am marrying Gerd. I'm marrying Gerd, as a grown man marries a woman.

The headache spreads like white light in a room, and she listens to her breathing. He lifts her head from his thigh and crouches down beside the bed. I don't know what to do, he says. She stares at him without expression.

Are you there? He snaps his fingers in front of her face. Folkví! She blinks. You need to pull yourself together now. He presses a hard kiss to her cracked lips, a jet of breath finding her nostrils. Crossing the long-room, he bends his neck and wipes his brow with his forearm. She sits up in the bed and slaps her hands down on the covers. I will not pull myself together! she shouts after him. What if I won't pull myself together? Without answering, he throws up his arms and shoves the door open. A moment later, she hears his voice and Od's outside, though she is unable to make out what they're saying, their words no more than a murmur in the wall.

The First Birth

She tried to focus. Fully dressed but for her feet, she had needed only to put on socks and shoes before she could set out, but then she'd ground to a halt. Her feet were buried in one of the sheepskins on the floor, her toes gripping the tufts and releasing, over and over. She stared at them. They were bony and bare in the tired brown wool, the big toes with their broad stubby nails inclining toward the rest of the flock, the little toes, outermost, weak-looking. That same sheepskin had been by the fireplace always, at least for as long as she could remember. Yes. She had wriggled her feet into it as a child, with someone holding her hand, because she couldn't yet stand or walk on her own: her tiny hands gripping an adult forefinger as she toddled her way forward. It wasn't something she really remembered, but she could see it in her mind. Her mother, young, in a long, light-colored dress, and although her face was blurred, the mood around her was quite vivid. She could sense her mother, and the family that once was, clearly. The sounds of the house when they were still children, the crackle of the fire, the spitting fat, and the low mumble of the servants, but also the family itself. When they ate or spoke, their footsteps on the floor, their sighs and yawns. To lie in the pool of sunlight from the open door and let everything meld into one, because you're home. The beat of a pulse in the hollow of her mother's neck. There'd been a different, closer warmth in the room then, and a particular way their parents had of speaking together, softly and with intimacy. She and Áslakr couldn't get through to them then, and didn't try. They would lie in the new straw, lost in play in the dark corner, while there, in the middle of the room, illuminated by the fire, their parents would sit talking hushed, that was the word for it, amid the smell of roasting pork. Folkví could sense them from the corner of her eye.

There was a way in which everything had seemed right, as long as they lived. The beds, when lined by their mother, were lined just right. There was an authority in all that she did, everything looked the way it was supposed to. When she wound her hair around her fingers and tightened it with the movement of a woman, the clip held between her pursed lips. And when, bent over at the waist, she would run after Áslakr, extending her arms toward him, fingers outstretched, tickling the air, Áslakr would jump and shriek and scramble to escape. This too was something Folkví could only imagine, having yet to be born when he was so little. And yet she had an idea of him, all the way back to when he'd been an infant, there was something about him that was him and that had been there always, it had remained unchanged through time. What he was to become, his long arms and legs, the exaggerated air of responsibility, it had all been present even then, albeit concealed. This was what she thought that morning, with her feet in the sheepskin, that for the most part he couldn't have turned out any different. The only things that could be changed were those that happened by chance. He could be seduced this very summer by a woman out on the point, for instance. He could get her pregnant. It was only a matter of whether he controlled the situations he got himself into, or they controlled him. When Folkví held an infant in her arms, she would sometimes think how the child differed from Áslakr, she would try to divine the essence of that particular baby and how he would have been by comparison. That each of them would grow up to live a life, just as Áslakr and she had, was incomprehensible to her. To think, the world was full of separate beings, each with its own life arc. It was a chaos into which she could plunge and vanish, and immediately she dismissed it from her mind. Áslakr was sitting on the bench watching her, there he was right now, with a smile on his lips. You're lost in thought, Folkví, he said. Shouldn't you get going? She smiled back at him. Yes.

She bent down and rolled up the sheepskin. She would take it with her today, for the baby to lie on after the delivery, why shouldn't she? People would accept whatever she proposed, they wouldn't question her. She tied a pouch of lavender and hair to her belt and pulled on her socks and shoes. Áslakr squeezed her arm. You'll do fine, he said, straightening her cloak. Around her neck she hung a key on a chain, then she pushed open the door. It was a special day, she could feel it in her entire body.

The young man who had come to wake her early that morning, while the moon was still up, had said his wife was almost ready. It was her second pregnancy, but this would be her first child, and his nervous energy, which put her in mind of a hunting dog, attentive to every sound, his movements quick and abrupt, had made a sharp contrast with Folkví, who'd stood with her hands tucked into her armpits, blinking drowsily, until the full import of what he was saying sank in. This was the first birth she'd been called out to since her mother's death. The first time she was to facilitate on her own. It was this sudden realization that snapped her awake. His wife was already showing the first signs of labor, the man said, and glanced quickly over his shoulder. But who knows, maybe it'll be hours yet before it really gets started. Who knows? He spat on the ground at his side and blew into his hands, his eyes darting this way and that. His right foot scuffed at a hard clod, are you coming then or not? Can we count on it? Our first child didn't survive the birth. Just so you know. The same sudden glance over his shoulder, a twist of his neck, and Folkví had to grip the doorframe. He counted out the pieces of copper in front of her with eyes that were bloodshot and inflamed, while she exhaled clouds of white and shivered. It was incredible. Frost already!

When she steps out into the morning with the sheep-skin rolled up under her arm, the sky has turned sharp and orange. The grass under her feet crunches with the frost, a silvery glaze. Before leaving she managed only to nibble a few bits of bread, they swelled in her mouth, and now her stomach aches, her teeth chatter. She holds the cloak aside as she mounts Munin, then clicks her tongue, urging the horse forward with a dig of her heels, then bumping along in the saddle as she passes the headman's house, the storehouses and stables. She grips the reins in one hand and nods to those she meets: hirdmen and young girls. Slanting rays of sunlight drench an old oak, moss-covered on one side, and its green is unreal in the clear morning, shining back at her. For a brief moment it draws everything else toward it. The long days to come, and a stillness rises around her. She fixes her eyes on the way ahead and prepares for her arrival.

She will present herself to whoever is there, with a smile. Although she is very young, she will carry herself with confidence and use the deeper register of her voice when she speaks. She will laugh reassuringly, disarm-ingly, to make them feel at ease with her. But the thought makes her feel dizzy, and she must remind herself: I've attended many births. I know the routine. Open all doors and shutters in the house. Administer the mandrake extract and invoke the aid of Frigg, so that the loins of the laboring woman may be unlocked. There will be a helping-woman, so while I may be important, I won't be the one receiving the child, the hands that will touch the woman's flesh will not be mine. It's a gift. The grunting woman, the stench, the blood. The blood will smear the arms of someone other than me.

Her eyelids droop and close. The sway of the horse, its broad, rhythmic movements, travels through her loins, a warmth against the insides of her thighs, cold air penetrating her face and hands. Her woolen undergarments prickle. She leaves the headman's yard through the gate and rolls her eyes to stay awake. The landscape is flat and pale, the orange light is higher in the sky and is fading to a thin yellow. She could break into a trot here in the open land, feel the horse's strength, as if to get the day going, but she won't. There's no reason to arrive early, for once she's there she won't be able to get away until it's over. They'll be grateful to see her no matter what, she'll step in, do something, make something happen, a difference. This time right now, before it starts, while she's still on her way, she'd like to prolong. In a day and a night it'll all be over. But now, as the horse beneath her rolls from side to side, as they follow the path to the village, past swathes of withered green and dry grass, it has not begun, not yet, it lies in wait.

The helping-woman stands outside the house, scanning, a hand shielding her eyes from the sun. Everything about her exudes efficiency and impatience, and Folkví feels an urge to veer away. It's not how she imagined it, the woman looks so severe. A flock of crows rises from the top of a tree, swooping away into the sky, and someone has already disheartened her. She balks at the day before her, not wishing to enter it like this, she would rather stay away and go muck around down at the fjord, keeping company with herself and people she knows. But there's a tense excitement too. She jumps down from her horse and leads it toward the helping-woman, takes a deep breath. She reviews the procedure in her mind: First the mandrake, next the doors and shutters. Then, an empty void. She can't remember the rest.

The helping-woman is at most ten years older than Folkví. Mousy hair twisted into a braid, narrow, pallid lips, keen eyes. Her face is bloodless, washed out. Broad at the waist and shoulders, though quite flat from the side. An instinctive animosity rises in Folkví, the woman's body language alone makes her feel she knows her already, the embodiment of every tight-lipped welcome she's received in her life. Eyes that size her up with skepticism, where she'd been hoping to pull through on charm: had trusted that everything was going to work out fine, that engaging with these strangers would be seamless, without her being able to say afterward exactly how she did it. Her nervousness would transform into a sense of being in the middle of it all, *it* being life and the world, no longer apart from people but together with them and glad, not least about herself. A person can have such charm when they first unfold and find their stride. But instead Folkví looks at this woman, and the eyes that look back at her are hesitant and silent, and so any confidence she may have felt is swept away: These are eyes that only want to see through you. Chatter and wildly gesticulating will cut no ice with me. Can you even do anything? That's the only thing that counts. And the question itself contains the answer: no, she can't. Not like that, on those terms, not if she has to prove it. Then she can do nothing, and she feels her body weaken. The woman looks at her blankly. You're the völva? she says. Folkví puts a hand to her throat, hoping it's not blotchy with blushing. Yes. She nods. Since my mother died it's just me. She is wearing one of her mother's old dresses, which is too big and a bit threadbare, wrinkled and not quite clean, she regrets it now, it makes her look much more disheveled out here in the world than she was at home, where she found its plainness appealing. She'd decided that its bagginess became her, that wearing it would bring her luck, she hadn't thought the moth holes and the faded fabric would matter that much. You seem in no hurry. Was there something else you had to do this morning? the woman asks. Folkví turns her necklace between her fingers and suddenly has no idea how she could have taken it all so lightly. No, she says after a moment. She breathes in. No, she says again. The woman stares at her. Her bright blue eyes give a withering glare, her head tipped back in disdain. I see, she says. You don't seem very together. With that, she turns and goes toward the house. Folkví tethers Munin and strokes her muzzle, her movements slow and stiff. I take it the birth hasn't started yet if you're standing out here, she says, her face half-buried in the mane. The helping-woman mumbles a no and goes inside. Then what's the problem? Folkví wonders. Tell me that.

By midday the birth still hasn't really gotten under way. The room is dismal and joyless. Folkví studies the young woman's unfamiliar, beastlike face, which has been taken over by a force more powerful than herself. Her eyes are tightly closed and she appears almost to be ruminating, her jaw making slow, disconcerting movements, a flat, high-pitched sound emanating from her, occasionally giving way to a howl. Then, with difficulty, she gets to her feet to stand with her hands pressed against a wall, roaring at the floor. The helping-woman stands with her, says something into her ear, and Folkví grows bored and sits down on a stool in the corner. An earthy, intimate smell mingles with the smoke of the fireplace, something leaks from the woman.

She didn't present herself quite the way she'd imagined when she entered, announcing instead, I'm here now, the völva. Two elderly, round-shouldered women looked up and nodded, she didn't catch who they were. On shaking legs, she'd stepped up to the bed and placed her hand on the woman's swollen abdomen in a manner of greeting, looking for something in her eyes, an ally perhaps, though finding nothing, the woman's face was puffy and she seemed completely absent, so Folkví simply lifted her head slightly and trickled the mandrake extract into her mouth. Swallow, she said softly, her fingers entangled in the woman's flat and sweat-drenched hair. The woman let out a cry and Folkví drew away too quickly, then glanced around and wiped her hands on the fabric of her dress. She felt the helping-woman's glare on her back as she stood there, a bit at a loss, her arms useless until she seized the initiative and made a beeline for a chest at the far end of the room. She rattled the lock, lifting the lid with much commotion, trying to come across as temperamental as possible, like someone who'd done this a hundred times before and more, a fearless person with a job to do. She stomped across the room, the soles of her feet slapping against the floor, and threw open all the doors and shutters with the same abrupt resoluteness. She snatched aside the curtain that was drawn in front of a sleeping bench. Finally, she pulled the front door wide open and breathed in, a pressing sensation in her chest, before stepping out into the white autumn air, her hand on the hinge. She heard the voice of the helping-woman inside the house. Folkví picked at her lower lip, removing flakes of skin, and allowed the air to cool her. She smoothed her faded blue apron dress with the palms of her hands and looked across at the neighboring house, where two older children were rolling a barrel.

Her mother had pulled the dress over her head, wriggling her sark into place underneath, smoothing the fabric until it sat evenly, pleasingly. The dress flared a little as it swept toward the ground, giving the impression that she was a legless being in shades of blue, a long, gliding movement with a head on top. She threw a thick purple woolen cloak around her shoulders, Folkví had never seen it before, closing it at the collarbone with two large silver brooches. It was a long cloak. The hands that carried out these tasks were practiced and lightly tanned by the sun. Rings of silver on every finger, reflecting the firelight, scintillating. My mother's hands twinkle, Folkví said to herself. She was sitting at the great long-table in the middle of the room watching, her feet couldn't reach the floor from the bench but dangled in thin air, her thighs tingling. The milk in her cup was tepid and Folkví slurped, a deep, hollow sound, a delightful gurgle, and she slurped again, this time on purpose and louder, she looked up from the cup and laughed. But her mother did not respond. She seemed preoccupied, removing a hair from her shoulder, Folkví couldn't keep her eyes off her. It was as if her mother sailed through the room as she went. Her head protruded stiffly from her cloaked frame, her hair falling about her expressionless face. There was something unfamiliar about the way she was that whole morning, and Folkví put her cup down with a loud clack. She slipped from the bench and jumped back into bed, it was good and warm, and she said something into Áslakr's ear. He was still asleep.

The sleet settled on the cloak in little pellets that quickly disloged again, the wool was clearly new. Its weave was thick and even, it was a fine cloak, as fine as nearly anything Folkví had seen, and she ran after her mother. Came up behind her out in the yard and reached out her hand, as quiet as could be she stroked the fabric and looked at her chubby hands against the purple wool. How nice it was. The cloak, so nice. When did you get it? she asked, stepping closer. But her mother simply laid her hand on Folkví's head. Njord, she called out to her husband, where are you? And Njord appeared then from the storeroom with a tub under his arm and looked at them serenely. Folkví and I are going now, she said. He nodded. See you before evening.

It was the first birth Folkví had attended, and the child had died. First it had screamed, then it had gone quiet. The woman howled and shouted, and Folkví stared at the dead baby in its mother's arms with no particular thought in her mind other than that it was ugly. A crumpled infant boy. Not at all adorable, like living infants with their tiny pink feet kicking pointlessly in the air. Later in the day her mother had offered the dead baby, sending it out onto the fjord in a little basket. As the basket took on water, a group of women stood singing. We give the child to Odin so as to please him, said her mother, smoothing Folkví's cheek, then clutched her tightly. Folkví drooled into the fabric at her mother's shoulder and made some sounds, heaving her own shoulders as if she were sobbing, and her mother pressed her hand against her back. There, there, Folkví, she said. A small beech tree grew at the offering place, and Folkví looked up into it, it swayed in the wind, and something about the whole scene was so splendid she felt like clapping.

Now there's a loud cry, and immediately Folkví gets

to her feet. The helping-woman doesn't even look at her as she comes across to stand beside her, all her attention concentrated on the birth. Folkví hesitates. She opens the flask of mandrake extract and holds it in front of the woman's face, the woman who is on her back, her legs splayed, fully present now, filled with aggressive energy. She hisses at Folkví as she tries to force the liquid into her mouth, and Folkví wheels away, stepping back a couple of paces into the dimness. She drinks from the flask, two mouthfuls in quick succession. A searing sensation runs down her throat into her chest. Her mother used to receive the child herself, with Folkví alongside her, and they would speak softly as the birth proceeded, Folkví assisting, fetching water, wiping and dabbing, occasionally she would receive the infant herself, her mother providing careful instruction. But things are much different now. She drinks a little more before putting the top back on, because there's the sheepskin, and in it some small residue of her mother's power. She can make ready to place the child on it, the way she intended, standing behind the helping-woman and watching the birth at a slight remove, and she can sing as it takes place, she knows a few birthing rhymes by heart. This can be her role, for surely she can't just leave . . . And so she positions herself a little apart from the others and opens her mouth the barest amount to sing. The voice that comes out of her is thin and trembling, a terribly frail sound. She persists, though she has started on too high a pitch, she can't hit the notes, her voice wavers. She trails away, as if the song were a sentence she'd begun without purpose that can only deteriorate into a mumble.

That was how it had been when her parents died, only a week apart. The same illness, the same brief course of events. First fever and diarrhea, followed by a period of violent spasms, then nothing: rattling, bony bodies, beads of sweat, a gradual departing of souls. Her mother died second, and Folkví had sat with her in the tent, though she had been told not to. She had clutched the small hand, tried to hold on to her mother's life, she no longer knew where to find solace. Never to see her face again, never to feel her hand against her neck, so deeply we attach ourselves to the physical body, the way it looks. The meaning a smile can convey, the particular twitch of an eye. She didn't want her mother ever to be put in the ground. In the days that led up to her death Folkví struggled to find words, tried to say goodbye, wanted to ask how they would manage, but the words wouldn't come, whenever she began a sentence it seemed treacherous, she was circling something she couldn't pin down, she interrupted herself, she stopped. When the body was put into the ship on a cold, rainy day, she wandered off into the woods as if she'd taken leave of her senses. The body, still the same, there was no way she could bring herself to see it covered up. She didn't have the strength to bear it.

Yes! the helping-woman yells, immersed in her work. Folkví puts her nose to the flask and breathes in, the room spins gently, she giggles and revives her song. She thinks she can see the infant's blood-smeared head now, appearing from the gaping vulva. Folkví sings without interruption, why not, no one is paying her any attention. She giggles again. It makes no difference, her being here. It won't be long now, the helping-woman says with a cackle, the birthing woman drawing up her legs, her face contorted, while the two elderly women help her up onto her elbows. Folkví struggles to contain her laughter, she tries to sing with more gusto, but her voice breaks and she lands on a wrong note. It is a ragged song, interminable. With every new verse it becomes more difficult to imagine how she can bring it to an end, as if she's gone too far to resolve it into a harmonic conclusion. But she's in the middle of it now, it seems impossible to stop, to stop would be to give in. I've found my own way of being here, and this is it. But if my mother saw me, the first time on my own, standing like an idiot in the corner . . . and she must go outside again and gulp in air. Everything she's learned and prepared for, it's gone, all the teachings of her childhood. She feels a twinge in her chest as she bends forward, tries to think of a funny way to relate it all to Áslakr later, and then starts laughing again. She hears the cries of a baby now. Folkví wipes her eyes. Before she leaves, head bowed, with flaming cheeks, she rolls up the sheepskin that without explanation has occupied the floor beneath the birthing woman, a detail she vows to remember, and she gives a little laugh in reverse, her breath drawn in rather than expelled.

Áslakr and one of the servants stand in hushed conversation as Folkví steps through the door. He breaks off. How did it go? She pushes off her shoes and unbuckles her cloak, tosses it over a bench. It didn't, she says, sitting down and removing the clip from her hair. It didn't go at all. Her hair tumbles around her shoulders, she smiles and looks away. I didn't know what to do without my mother.

Áslakr sits down, facing her on the bench, his forearms brought to rest on his thighs. The helping-woman didn't like me. All I could do was stand there useless. She looks up at him and tries to laugh. I sang really badly. But that's funny, isn't it? He studies her. I don't know, he says. But, Folkví. I've spoken to the headman today. He gets up and stirs the pot above the fire as if unwittingly, a soup simmering away. He scratches his elbow. I'm going on an expedition, he says. Folkví lifts her gaze and stares at his back. He thinks I'm ready, so you'll have the house to yourself all winter. She looks down at her hands, they lie cupped in her lap. When? she says. Áslakr clears his throat. It won't be for a while yet. We're going in a month and coming back in the spring. Folkví turns away, says nothing, again and again and again she must get back on her feet. She can't bear that they keep leaving her, one after another.

*

She is not allowed on expeditions. She won't see the seas when they swell out, how the world is vast and open and flat. No one knows what lies beyond the horizon. The wind tugging at their hair, the men in song, their deep grand choir, she could lie cocooned on the deck, swaddled in a white sheet, she could fall asleep there. The tallest waves would crash over the sides, salt water would slap her face. But she will see no action. She will remain at home with her combative desires. Restlessness quivers in her body, she goes to the loom and back again, recites rhymes, but her disquiet will not lift. She wonders, where is Áslakr? There is peace and dignity to be found in women's work, fingers brushing against coarse threads in the half-light, the weaving of great sails. The ships put out from the harbor and make away through the fjord. The others stand on the shore, the women, the children, the farmers, a farewell to lovers, brothers, and sons. This place is too small, tears run down the cheeks into the mouth that opens into a smile at the thought of everything new they will see, how much love a person can feel for her brother, and there he stands, small now, as the ship glides over the water, standing with his arms aloft, there stands my brother, and I love him. They return home the following spring with uncounted rugs and beads, items of silver and wooden figurines. Folkví goes to the market, she is wealthy and buys beautiful things she holds sacred in her fine home. Often she will stand back and admire them. Those glasses are just incredible.

A Small God

WINTER

Fatigue, the entire winter Áslakr is away on the expedition. It feels like the darkness will never let go of her, not for a moment. The cold is entrenched in the walls, it comes seeping from the recesses to skim her face in the night. Her head is heavy with this fatigue, even when she wakes. These deathly still mornings, with no Áslakr or any hirdmen to come or go, the disagreeableness of keeping house on her own, the thralls her silent witnesses. The sense of everything coming apart on her when he isn't there, she shuts herself in, hides away from the servants and uses her house as Freya uses her hall: at times for feasts that go on until early morning, at times totally closed off, her private space, until she barely remembers what expression to muster in order to say good morning, let alone to put someone to work. She doesn't know who she is then. She tosses her head, her hair tumbles down her back, and she gathers it against her breast. She combs it assidiously with the ivory comb, working her way up from the ends.

It was her hair that told her mother instantly that Freya was Folkví's god, for when she was born it wasn't sparse and wooly like the hair of most infants, but long and thick and lustrously golden, already covering her ears. You looked very special, her mother said when she recounted it to Folkví, a grown woman and a baby at the same time, you had small breasts that swelled even then. You looked like a small god. When subsequently her hair began to fall out in long tufts, her mother had gathered them up and put them in the leather pouch with dried lavender that now hangs from the belt Folkví wears around her waist.

With practiced movements Folkví parts her hair equally in two before she gathers herself and opens the door to call in one of the servants. Thora, the little churlish one, younger than Folkví, she played with her sometimes when they were children, comes hurrying after a moment, breathless, with fresh, ruddy cheeks. Folkví sits in silence on the stool as Thora's cold fingertips sift through her hair, until with an abrupt yank she begins to braid it. A small gasp escapes her, she closes her eyes and braces her neck against the girl's busy movements. Folkví is beautiful, Thora says with a lisp, twisting colored ribbons into her mistress's hair. Folkví smiles gratefully without opening her eyes. The roots of her hair seem almost to tingle, and she gathers her hands in her lap.

There's a new god, his name is White-Christ. She doesn't know what to make of it. He seems frail. Doesn't govern anything in particular, so when is she supposed to make offerings to him? He doesn't appear to her in visions either, is more like a muffled sensation now and then. Some of the journeying traders speak of him as if he were elevated above the Æsir. Presumably he doesn't know them. Where is he, if not in Asgard? Who are his brothers, who's he married to? What can he do? Some claim him to be the son of Odin. And a couple of days before Áslakr left with the expedition, he told of Francia and the incredible buildings they erect there to honor White-Christ, he said they sounded almost beyond belief, like nothing anyone had ever seen or imagined. But Folkví believes it to be true, the jewelry and vessels she has from there tell her so. They possess such exceptional refinement, as do the figurines from Arabia. Áslakr said there were those in the south who believe White-Christ to stand alone. That he is the wisest. He drew his sleeve across his mouth, and bread crumbs fell from his beard onto his shirt. They do this, he said, his mouth still full of food, and he moved his hand in the air: up and then down, to the side and across. I think it's instead of offering. It's like a sign. Folkví lay on the sleeping berth built into the side of the long-room, she arranged the skins and blankets so that she could turn on her side. She looked at her brother. Instead of offering? Yes, at least that's what the headman says. And when all those men fell, Trond apparently asked that the sign of White-Christ be made at their grave. Folkví had turned onto her back and gazed up then at the hole in the roof through which the thin smoke was drawn away, a sharp disk of blue. Did they do so? Yes. Or rather, they offered to Thor as well, so I suppose they thought it wouldn't harm.

Maybe it wouldn't, but still Folkví is uncertain about it. She can't get a handle on him. White-Christ. An ominous-sounding name, like a man standing in fog. Ill-defined, a blur. Does he rise up out of the fjord in the early morning? Dark green leaves, mist, a light rustle. But the image dissolves again. It's a different thing altogether from Odin, with his single narrow eye, dark and strong and pensive: she knows his gestures, his scheming character. Or Thor, with his big beard, his broad shoulders, his chestnut-colored hair. A pleasing, square face and laughing eyes. Thor, who could embrace a person with an enormous hand, draw them toward him, and they'd still feel safe as a child. Glad as one too. Odin's skin is cooler, grayer, he has slender hands. With him, you would recline elegantly on your side, pass your hand across his chest while he lay on his back, the straw would poke from between the sheepskins, and his all-seeing eye would study you for a time. More detached, not as warm. Intelligent. The two of you would speak more quietly and more earnestly. Not entwining until he would lean over her and, with an intensity quite different from before, sink his sinewy body down between your hips.

And Freya, who helps her the most, so light of heart and uncomplicated, one would think, yet in all her abundance and strength there is a sadness she bears. She delivers the fallen warriors to Valhalla, holds feasts in her hall, and is often the center of attention, being so beautiful and outgoing. But then she can grow bored all of a sudden, or her mood may turn dark, she will keep to herself and not leave Folkvang for days on end, plaintive cries may be heard from her house, and no one is allowed inside. And though she sleeps with nearly every man, there was a time once when she married, only for her husband to leave her after the wedding, and she flew all over the world in desperate search of him. She never found him. This side of Freya too is familiar to Folkví, she admires her for her strong will and her gentleness. Folkví makes offerings to Freya when she needs comfort. She knows Freya, but White-Christ is a stranger.

A sudden noise makes her jump. Oh, did I give Folkví a start? says Thora, her voice bright, and she bends down to retrieve the comb, a hand resting on Folkví's shoulder. Her touch has something consoling about it, like the assured gesture of a parent, and Folkví twists away, an abrupt movement that prompts Thora to remove her hand. No, Folkví replies, aware that the flatness of her tone betrays that she's upset. You interrupted me in my thoughts, that's all. Thora says nothing in reply, her fingers move smoothly and quickly through Folkví's loose hair, the same movements over and over again, soothing and unsettling. The girl's thumbs graze Folkví's ears, gentle upward movements, her fingers dissolving into the hair, softly massaging Folkví's scalp. It's an inappropriate and surprising act of solicitude in the lonely winter, and Folkví lifts her neck, stretches toward Thora's kindly caressing hands.

This morning she emptied the contents of a large jar onto the floor. She was missing Áslakr, in the first moments of waking had forgotten that she was alone, and then, deflated by his absence, had refused to get up at all. But then she got the sudden impulse to seek signs of his return, how long she had to wait, and though ordinarily she would have gone into the woods to look for clues in bark and roots, fatigue at the thought of wandering about out there, cold and directionless, looking for something she wouldn't recognize unless she found it, led her to the less complicated option of upending her jar of amulets and figurines. Averting her gaze, she hovered her hands above the scattered pile, her fingers and palms tingling, and when she looked down at the object she'd picked, she saw it was a small wooden medallion bearing an indistinct image of White-Christ. She ran her thumb over it, once only, before putting it aside with a shudder and hurriedly gathering the contents of the jar together again.

White-Christ is not a sign. He cannot be read, and therefore can be accorded no significance.

One day shortly after Áslakr's departure, there'd been a knock at the door. Outside stood an odd little man, a follower of White-Christ making his way north from Friesland through Sjælland. She bid him enter with a generous sweep of her hand and invited him to take a seat on a bench in the long-room, where she studied him expectantly. It was all rather exciting, she had no idea what might happen, what he would want from her, and the first thing he did was to produce from a leather pouch the wooden medallion with the image of White-Christ. A god impaled on a simple wooden cross. The god was dead, the Frisean told her, and she looked at the figure's head, which was drooped to one side. He couldn't have much power then, Folkví reasoned. He looked more like a sacrificed thrall than anything else. Indeed, said the Frisean, indeed. He has sacrified himself for the good of man. Folkví tilted her head. She felt like laughing and drinking, in reverse order. No, she said. The only god to have sacrificed himself was Odin, and he did so to learn the runes: he hanged himself from a tree, after which he lived on, knowing the magic of the runes. But this god, why would he offer himself up? For what purpose? And before the Frisean managed to get a word in: It doesn't make sense at all, why would a god sacrifice himself to us people? Wasn't that what he'd just said? Was this god so grateful for being worshipped that he offered himself to his worshippers? What kind of nonsense is that, what kind of meaningless act, do the gods now believe that men are gods? He comes here and speaks as if the world were turned on its head. *What kind of a god would sacrifice himself?* And who would make sacrifice to a god who is no stronger than that? Who, she exclaimed finally, her voice having risen to a shout, could possibly find use for a god who is dead? And with that she went outside to one of the stores and fetched a jug of wine, she was trembling and the glasses chinked in her hand, but she collected herself, came back inside, and poured for them both. Bottoms up, she said in a voice that was far too loud, and sniggered, raising her glass to the Frisean with a nod and a glance. He sipped politely, perched on the edge of the bench.

He spoke with a heavy accent and looked at Folkví quizzically every now and then. He wasn't very tall, and sat with his back straight and his hands folded at his knees, his glass placed discreetly on the floor between his feet.

His face was peculiar. Its features were small, as if squashed together in the middle, under strong, deep-set eyes. The fire crackled, and with slight hesitation he proceeded to tell her about a poor infant boy born a long time ago without benefit of intercourse, a miracle. He was extremely poor, the man repeated several times, as if that were a good thing. There was something about him that both attracted and repelled Folkví, she felt somehow sorry for him and took care not to interrupt, nodding often to show that she understood. He told her the new god gave the dead a place to go if you worshipped him, and looked as if he regretted the words even as he spoke them—as if the need to speak and the aversion he felt toward doing so coincided—and yet he persisted, there were a number of points still to be made. In a voice that was now almost a whisper, he leaned toward her and told her this god was in truth half man. While he was speaking, Folkví had become absorbed in the little image, already somewhat sympathetic to the new god, if that was what he was. Not very strong. Rather childlike. His face was long and oddly frail-looking. He didn't look at all like Odin, and Folkví was confused, the wine made her feel strange, as if she was concentrating, though on what she didn't know, and she just sat in dreamy silence when eventually the Frisean got to his feet. He asked to make the sign of his god in front of her chest. She did nothing to stop him, but remained seated on the bench as his long, thin fingers drew the cross of White-Christ in the air before her. Afterward she showed him to the door, where they said farewell without really looking at each other. He came back the next day wanting to carry on their conversation, but this time she instructed one of the servants to send him away.

Thora steps away from Folkví with satisfaction. There, Folkví's as fine as can be. Good, Folkví says, and Thora dips at the knee and turns to leave, but Folkví stops her before she scurries away. Would you get Munin ready? I'm going to the market. Yes, of course, Thora says, and smiles tentatively. If Folkví wishes, I could go with her. She stands with her hands clasped behind her back, an open expression on her face. Folkví looks at her. This behavior, teetering between that of a servant girl and a free woman, is at least in part her own doing, as one day in summer she'd pressed a small clay bead on a leather cord into Thora's hand on their way home from Lejre, where Folkví had been called to drive out a sickness. Folkví had taken only Thora with her, on the very first day a young man had died in her hands. That evening, she and Thora had drunk together in the tiny room they had been given, and talked about their childhood until the first light. She had fallen asleep with an arm around Thora's waist, and the next evening Thora had been waiting on Folkví's bed when she entered the room. How did it go today? Thora had asked, her voice mild and chirpy. It went well, Folkví replied. Now undo my dress for me. Thora had asked no further questions, and Folkví hadn't spoken either. Not until they lay down together for the night, back to back, did she feel like telling Thora how much better she had done that day, but by then their silence had become a barrier between them, a wall that could not be scaled. Thank you, Folkví says now, some other time perhaps, but it won't be necessary today. She glances at the girl. The clay bead rests against her collarbone, above her simple gray dress, and rises as she breathes.

Munin's great nostrils widen as Folkví tethers the horse to a post on the outskirts of the market and runs her hand over its muzzle a couple of times. She pulls back her hood to reveal her intricate braids and walks the last bit of the way. Already she can hear the sounds of the market, the smith's pounding of metal on metal, the murmur of voices, the livestock protesting their tethers, and up ahead she sees the first tents, where fish and skins may be had. A large fire has been lit in front of the pit houses where the fishing families and artisans are housed, sparks fly upward. The fire cracks against the sky, the gray sky.

Some young men stand gathered in a group, a couple of them call out to her—hey, Folkví—and as she turns her head to respond, her eyes latch on to an unfamiliar face. In the midst of these boisterous young men, all of whom she knows—they grew up at Frøsted, grew up in its fields, their faces marked by all those days of hard work, creased by the sun, their bodies lean and wiry—in their midst stands a young man unknown to her. His impassive gaze lingers on her a moment, his frame rugged and unmoving in the lively throng, and she stiffens, for there's something about him, she's seen him before, but can't remember where. She scans various places in her mind, places she's been, maybe he's a trader she bought something from, or maybe he's from a neighboring town, and then it comes to her. The solstice celebration in the headman's hall years before . . . She feels herself weaken at the knees and straightens her back. The first time she saw him he'd simply disappeared, a traveler she'd never see again. But something about him had interested her immensely, and here he is once more, older now and more of a man, but also the same. Clothes of a coarse woolen cloth. He folds his arms, tucking his hands into his armpits, his eyes follow her as she passes. Further along the path she stops at one of the stalls. Exquisite beads, a jug, darkly glazed, she runs her hand over it. Soon the stranger is behind her, quite close behind, and her entire back hums.

At the woodworker's, daylight streams in through the entrance and the big smoke hole above the fire, but apart from that the interior is dim. She sees the stranger's silhouette in the doorway, hears him speak with the peasant boys, and turns quickly away, blushing, but she is only in half-light, then asks the woodworker how he's coming along with the box she's commissioned. She's speaking too quickly. She feels the beating of her heart. A couple of days and it'll be finished, as they agreed. The woodworker scratches his graying beard and spits to the side. He circles the big wheel he's fixed at the lathe, runs a chisel along its edge. Folkví smiles at him, though with his back half turned he's oblivious, she tries to think of something more to say but can't, so she stands there a moment. The woodworker leans over the wheel and starts sanding it, then pauses to peer up at her, eyebrows raised, with a look that says, was there anything else? I'll come back then, she says, and bends to pick up the basket she's put down on the floor. Good, he says, already returned to his work.

Folkví hangs the basket over her arm and is almost at the doorway before she again hears the deep voice of the stranger outside, his laughter, and she dallies. Now she can see him from his rear flank. She pauses and puts down her basket. She crouches, rummages through its contents as if there's something she can't find, as if confused, which in actual fact she is, she removes a couple of items and puts them down on the floor: a shawl, a hunk of bread, a bunch of nettles she plucked along the way. She senses the woodworker looking up again from his work. Everything all right? he wants to know. There's annoyance in his voice. Yes, she mutters back, it's just—and the sentence is left hanging, she mumbles something inaudible and feels the warmth return to her cheeks. The woodworker says no more. Hurriedly she gathers her things together, bites the skin above her thumbnail, compelled now to get to her feet and leave. And all the while, she hears the lively voices outside, feels the warmth in her, even in her palms, her heart beating in her chest, why is she so flustered? She straightens up and stands, oddly positioned in the middle of the room, but she will not move, the stranger has command of her legs, they go weak—will she be able to walk past him and just stare at the ground, will she be able to cover her face, her burning cheeks—well, goodbye then, enjoy the day, she says, and turns to look at the woodworker one last time. And then with a nod of his head he indicates a bench, you can sit there, if there's something you need to sort out. She smiles, whispers a word of thanks. He shrugs.

It's an awkward situation, but she feels she must accommodate the woodworker in some way. They know each other, at least slightly, the way people do at Frøsted, she sits there on the bench and makes conversation. The words rise inside her and bubble from her mouth, she is visited unexpectedly by joy. She has come here all her life more or less, her father was always fond of the woodworker, does he remember her father? Of course, he says. He has taken the wheel from the lathe and put another in its place. Her father found the woodworker to be a man of impressive bearing, or did he? Somehow the words don't seem right, but nonetheless it's what she says: that as a little girl she loved to come to the marketplace with her father, and in particular how she loved to come to the woodworker's workshop—how she loved to come here. Perhaps he wasn't aware of that. Well, maybe not, now you mention it. He pauses and looks at her, wipes his brow with the back of his hand, a little skeptical maybe, but he's softening, she can tell. And she continues, she and Áslakr, her brother, does he know her brother? Anyway, they were always wanting to impress their father, she laughs, so one time they'd played at being woodworkers, pretended they were the woodworker and their father, to make their father happy, and she laughs again and her eyes sparkle. Isn't that funny? The woodworker smiles sheepishly, yes, perhaps it is. What was it she said, just so he's sure of it, she's Njord and Ingvild's daughter, is that right? That's it, yes. Well, there you are, then. He was an important figure at Frøsted, Njord. You never really think a person notices you, apart from family and the like, of course, but he has to say, he was a great supporter of Njord. Yes, Folkví bursts out, and it was mutual, I can tell you! Her father was a much simpler man than many people thought, or maybe that's not the way to put it, but he was unsentimental, yes, and Folkví believes there was something about the woodworker's way that he appreciated. The woodworker never made pretenses, that was always plain. And a lot of people probably thought Njord was a bit superior and never took proper notice, a man immersed in his own affairs, but he saw what was in people, he did. She smiles and gesticulates, and in the woodworker especially. She embarks on a long story about the time her father returned home from an expedition, all the things he'd missed about Frøsted, and it was a lot, the children, their mother, the food, the particular light that came off the fjord, but also the way people were in the town, like the woodworker. Some people aren't always on their way to somewhere else. Her father had been all over the place, but he appreciated the things that stayed the same. It's just as important as going on expeditions, he said, yes, as important even as being the headman, he said so himself, often. Her brother's exactly the same. And she can't halt her words, doesn't even think of halting them until much later, that evening when she reflects, in the moment she's simply so filled up with joy.

She has risen to her feet and stepped over to look at his work. He tells her about the rounding of the wheel, how the wood must be soaked in water to become pliable, amenable to being worked, he runs his hand over the spokes, feel this. But as she places her hand on the smooth wood, a shadow passes across the doorway and she hears the voice of the stranger, hey there, he says. Then, his heavy footsteps on the workshop floor as he comes toward them, as he emerges from the shaft of light into the semidarkness his features become clearer. There's something boyish about his appearance now. His long bangs falling in front of his eyes, his back almost exaggeratedly broad. He doesn't look at her. The woodworker steps away from Folkví and wrings his hands in his apron, his face opening into a smile—hey, Od, he says, and Folkví feels the name resonate inside her: Od! Such a sound. A short sound, a good fit for a solid face. Dear child, I call you Od. And an Od the child became. Or like the sound of a cooking pot, if softly chanted, Odddd—Oddddd, a sound that would induce a trance, because it's so simple. Od is the soothing sound of metal.

The woodworker has gone out to fetch Od's order. Od stands next to her, quietly, her hand still rests on the light-colored wood. He places his own beside hers, barely a few thumb-lengths from the work, a gigantic hand by comparison, it looks like a thick, yellowy film of wax has encased the skin, which is quite white and cracked at the extremities. She stares at it. Here and there, dark bristles poke from large, open pores.

The Summer of the Offering

There's a time for calamity, when the sun goes black in the long hot summer, when the harvest fails, when two ships capsize. But the lull, when things have not yet gone wrong and the sun may still rise and everyone laugh with relief and make grateful offerings, is a time not of calamity but of tiny, fluttering hope. It is the moment the runes are cast and hang suspended in the air. Who does one call upon to secure the most favorable outcome?

Od and Áslakr look sideways at each other. Is that what we do, then? Od says. Áslakr nods and leans back against the outside wall, to drench his face in sunlight. Maybe it's best all around that she doesn't come to the wedding. They stand in silence. In the yard in front of them a black cat with white paws arches its back and curls

around a handcart, its tail slipping between the spokes.
The cats have always been Folkví's, as the sparrows were
their mother's. Áslakr watches it for a moment. It sits
down in the shade of the tipped cart and licks a paw, absorbed in its own life. It's a little thing, he senses, not quite
fully grown, and he has to look away. It would place a
mouse proudly at his feet, he imagines, and in a way
Folkví's like that too. Sweet, in her helpless attempts to
look after herself. Irritating and at the same time touch-
ing in her need to be recognized and appreciated, from as
far back as when they were children: Look what I managed. Didn't I do well? And then you have to praise her
and put all your attention on her, and hardly ever have the
chance to talk about your own successes. Now he and Od
have agreed that Folkví is to be driven out to the pasture
where the helping-woman will rid her of her darkness—
the helping-woman and time itself, for time too must do
its share: Folkví is to stay there until the evil is gone from
her. Áslakr feels like a traitor, not just to her but to his
family. Sending his only sister away before the wedding.
But he doesn't know what else to do, there's a force in her
that won't let go, and it must. She won't eat, will barely
speak, her eyes gleam gray behind a milky-white film,

then they spill over again. She stares and weeps, and he was shocked when he lifted the blanket from her earlier. That bony frame isn't hers, not at all soft and inviting. Her skin has taken on a tinge of yellow.

Od shifts his weight onto his other foot. I think I'll get going, he says. Áslakr wrenches himself from his thoughts. He looks at Od, who bends his head and pinches his nose a couple of times. Sometimes he can lose himself completely and will stand as if transfixed, an elbow cupped in one hand, the tip of his nose pinched between the thumb and forefinger of the other like this while he stares at the ground. Áslakr likes that about him. It's a thoughtful and conscientious man who pauses in such a way, caught up in some inner dialogue, he imagines: Should he stay or go? Should he give in to his urge to take care of Folkví or not? Sometimes Áslakr will even see him swipe the air in front of him, as if to wave away one argument with another, thinking himself unseen. Go, for she barely knows you're here. Or else, I can't go now, not when she needs me. This is Od's struggle, to contend against himself: The fickle solicitude of the rejected, what is to be done with it? Yes, Od now says, as if to settle the matter once and for all. Yes, says Áslakr. Be off, by all means. He clamps his hand on Od's shoulder and gives it a squeeze, and Od turns away, buries his hands in his pockets. Áslakr stands and watches him as he crosses the yard. A dark figure, hunched as if to protect himself, the dry earth kicking up in dusty clouds about his feet. Áslakr steps away from the wall, the afternoon is deadeningly hot.

The brown tones are unpleasantly familiar. The smell too, a hint of bark. At the bed, one of the servant girls, Thora, turns Folkví on her side. Áslakr watches her. She comes across as cheerful and self-reliant, handling Folkví's frame with an ease that seems natural and unconcerned, lifting her head further up the pillow, neither heavy-handed nor overly affectionate. A fleeting desire passes through him, for Thora to come and redeem him, to run her hand uncomplicatedly through his hair until he finds composure. He collects himself and greets her. Hey, Thora. His voice is a tad too deep, he clears his throat. Leaning over Folkví, she looks up at him and smiles, hey, she says. Just a moment and I'll be done. Unlike the other servants she seems not at all afraid to be in the house, there's a bond of some sort between her and Folkví that Áslakr can't quite fathom. Maybe she helps Folkví with her sorcery, who knows. But last summer, when Folkví without a hint of explanation went off into the woods and stayed there, he had availed himself of her particular disposition.

For a time after the deaths of their parents, Folkví rode out with increasing frequency to their burial mound to spend the night there and channel the omens. He had refrained from interfering, it was a natural response, and it was only when one time she still hadn't returned by the next afternoon that he rode out to the place himself. He found her sitting cross-legged on top of the mound, the hood of her blue cloak pulled up over her head, the whites of her eyes showing as she mumbled softly to herself in an unfamiliar language. Folkví, he called, with no other response than an abrupt twist of her neck, as if to ward off a troublesome insect, and no pause in her mutterings. He had ridden back home, but when darkness fell and she still hadn't returned, he went there again, passing through the woods at a gallop so as not to be seized by their beings, and found her in the same place as before, the same eyes turned skyward, only now chuckling to herself as she babbled on in her indecipherable language. She kept turning her face in different directions, pausing at intervals as if engaged in discussion with a number of parties who were all to be given time to speak. Áslakr watched her from a distance.

Clearly, she was greatly engaged, listening attentively without moving, her hands on her knees, her upper body inclined slightly forward—but toward what, the leaves and the animals?—and then she laughed, the blankness of her face giving way. Throughout the night he watched his sister, perched cautiously with his back against a tree, the bushes rustling, and for a brief moment she turned her unseeing eyes in his direction and smiled. It was a slow, deliberate smile, as if delivered through the soil from some other age. Then she turned back to others again.

Áslakr listened to the woods that night. Trees creaked, and creatures emerged, rabbits, birds, and deer gathering at the foot of the mound, approaching warily, then settling. Every now and then Folkví sang snatches of melody in a high-pitched voice, and the animals pricked up their ears. In the early morning Áslakr rode home again, the woods dew-drenched, the first light soft and yellow among the trees, the sun and the dizzying fatigue he felt made him empty and serene, and as he sat on his horse it was as if he fell headlong out of himself. At last he entered the headman's yard, where Thora was the first of the servants he saw, and he asked her to go to the burial place and put out food for Folkví—not to interrupt her in her communion, not to ask questions, but simply to leave the food there for her on the mound where she sat. In the days that followed, Thora carried out this task without objection, only once did Áslakr go himself. He couldn't look at Folkví there. An anger at her absorption flared inside him: at first he was scared, but then he grew annoyed. It was like she was deliberately turning away from human life and exaggerating the communication in which she was engaged. As if something in her preferred the company of the dead and the animals, how oppressive it all was.

When finally she came home after thirteen or fourteen days, she was filthy and tired, but happy. Mother and Father are well, she said cheerily, and was quite herself again. But now I'll sleep. She splashed her face with water and ran a cloth over it. The rest can wait. All I want is to get out of these clothes and into bed and close my eyes, she said, and kissed his hair. The next morning she got up early and washed properly, put on clean clothes, she was radiant and set about carving runes into her staff, her good spirits unabated. When Áslakr with some disquiet asked her what she'd learned on the burial mound, all she said was: Ah. Was there anything in particular you wanted answered? You should have told me before I went, and with that she gave a shrug and turned her attention back to her runes.

Thora gets up from the bed. There you are, she says, making room for Áslakr. I can give Folkví some food tonight, if Áslakr wishes. Thanks, Áslakr says. We'll see, if you'd mind waiting outside? Thora closes the door behind her, and he turns to Folkví and looks down at her. Her face is still yellow. This is what's going to happen, he says quietly. Tomorrow Od and I will come with the helping-woman. We'll take you out to the pasture, where there's a tent you'll stay in until this unwelcome force has been driven out. It's for your own good, for the good of everyone, I'd say. It seems only to be getting stronger. And you're too far from Utgard here, whatever it is that's got into you, it'll have to walk home on its own.

Look at me, he says then.

. . .

Do you know how mad it makes me when you don't answer?

Folkví listens to Áslakr. To get rid of her while the wedding takes place, that's what he wants. He's turning his back on a side of himself, trying to live with one eye shut. There was a time when together they were the most adventurous of all the children in the headman's yard. Now he wants rid of her. But he has known her always, she's a part of him. If something was strong, it must remain so, of this she is certain.

Áslakr stretches his limbs as if for something to do while staring at the ceiling. Eventually he sits up, shifts himself to the edge of the bed, and leans forward to put on his shoes, only Folkví won't have it, cannot bear to see him put on shoes and get ready to leave her, turning to face the world. Áslakr, she says, but he says nothing in reply, sits quietly for a moment while picking something from between his lips, then slips a foot into a shoe. She says his name again, Áslakr, and he grunts, what?, throws her a look of annoyance. I don't know, she breathes, won't you stay? No, he says, and gets to his feet. She grabs his thigh and pulls him toward her, to stop him from leaving. Let go. His voice is calm, but she holds on and whispers again, Áslakr. And he turns then, a sudden movement toward her. She releases him, his crotch is poised above her face, she holds her breath, is she seeing what she's seeing? She can smell him, and he forces her down. He turns her over and pulls up her sark, baring her buttocks, holds her still with a hand against the back of her head as he penetrates her. When she tries to look over her shoulder and into his eyes, he twists his hand around her hair, tightens his grip, and she can't move her head. But on the edge of her vision she senses his face, dogged and concentrated, and he has closed his eyes.

Sometimes when she sees Áslakr from a distance she finds herself suddenly aware that his legs are too long. That odd sway of his hips, does he waddle? She studies his predictable gestures, the way his movements have become adult and normal, the way he listens sympathetically to even the tritest of opinions, his brow furrowed in a frown. But close up all of this is gone, and she sees him once again the way he is, the part of him that breaches time and remains constant. That is when she reaches out, or wishes to while her hands remain in her lap. He is the true Áslakr then. It resides in his face, who would he be without his face, it's how he expresses himself, through the features of his family, the boyish smile. It's his spirit too that's so moving. The way he had to fight for things when he was little, his serious demeanor, the care he took, like the time he'd made a knife for his father and then wouldn't present him with it, even though he'd been working away at it evening after evening. His courage failed him, and Folkví hadn't understood a thing, but jumped up and down: Father, he's made you something. Yes, you have! She still wells up at the thought of Áslakr's little potbelly, his downcast eyes, he'd been embarrassed at having made such an effort. All this too is embedded in his face, when it suddenly becomes open and bewildered.

He left her with semen up her back. Folkví wipes it away with a blanket and sits back against the wall. There is a violence in Áslakr that she guards. His face, the way he let go of her hair and looked at her, almost with disdain, she thinks with satisfaction, because now he has recognized himself. She calls Thora in and asks her to obtain an assortment of hearts. She opens the leather pouch that's hidden under the pillow and takes out a piece of silver, presses it into Thora's hand, and blushes. The way he grabbed hold of her, his small, open mouth at the end. Somewhere deep down there is an objection she ignores. He is the one who must never turn and leave.

★

In the summer a dry smell of grain may hang in the air. And later in the year, when the harvest has been taken in, the stubble is stiff and sharp, and woe to whoever ventures into the field barefoot. If the soles are not toughened, the strong spikes may penetrate the fine skin of the arch in particular. She cuts easily and would never be able to flee across a field without shoes, not in summer, not in autumn, not in winter. Perhaps in spring, when the young shoots emerge soft and grasslike from the lumpy soil. The newly turned earth, when the seed has just been sown, surely she would be able to run on that. And her legs would feel strong, her thighs tingling as she reached speed, arms pumping in counterpoint to the legs, her skirt hitched up and tied around her waist so that she could run as fast as possible. For all her might. It's good to be a young woman with strong thighs, and it's good to use the body and to trust the soil into which the heels embed, though it may conceal shards of flint. Flint cuts so cleanly it doesn't even hurt at first.

The Summer of the Offering

Thora bends forward and eases Folkví down onto the bed. She's brought with her a stew of pigeon hearts and waits now for it to work, for Folkví to succumb, so that she can withdraw. She intones the verse Folkví has requested, *I will show you the way into a dream. There is victory in your breast and a victory in your hand.* She looks into Folkví's pale face as she says the words. Folkví's lips are lightly parted, her eyes not quite shut, her body as if abandoned, sloughed off. Occasionally she gives a little start, a whimper escapes her or she moves her head slightly, but Thora can tell she's drifting further and further away. Her mouth has fallen open, her head dropped to the side, a thin dribble of spit travels down her cheek.

As Thora repeats the same verse over and over, she thinks of her new prosperity. Áslakr has paid her with

silver to keep quiet about Folkví. Folkví has paid her to
come to her tonight. The headman will pay her to report
to him in the morning on Folkví's condition. Altogether,
she does the sums in her head as she recites, altogether she
will have twelve pieces of silver, maybe more, by the time
the week is out. And if Folkví will only set her free in
thanks for her loyalty—if only she will, and why not,
when she's almost said as much already?—she'll be able to
find herself a free man, a home of her own at Frøsted. She
dreams of wearing the key to a house on a chain around
her neck. Pictures it all in her mind: the little house, mod-
est but good. On the outskirts of the settlement, all right,
but she's not afraid of the woodland beings or of hard
work. A single room, how long and how wide? And then
at one end . . . what, a stable? Could she keep a cow? She
imagines skins and blankets, a wooden chest for clothes.
Sleeping berths along the wall, for siblings, uncles, children. The way their breathing will separate into different
rhythms in the darkness, as she herself lies awake and listens. She sees too a loving man, an honest man. What is
he like? A little younger? But she knows already who it
could be. It could be Gisle. She smiles. Gisle, the way he
pronounces his words so clearly, always sticking to the

subject at hand, never one to make waves. Gisle, who as a child lost his arm above the elbow and yet, tirelessly and without drama, works in the field, fishes at the stream, gesticulating with the stump that remains: insistent on being precise, not caring to be entertaining. And if a conversation doesn't suit him, if people are incoherent, their words ill-considered, he will lower his gaze. He will not laugh if something isn't funny. Thora realizes she isn't singing anymore but merely humming, slowly, absently, snatches of the melody. She slips a hand inside her undergarment, watchful of Folkví with her yellow pallor: She is asleep. Her eyelids flutter comically. And though it's a sign that Thora may leave, she curls her fingers stealthily as she imagines pulling off Gisle's shirt, straddling him, and her loins constrict, this is all it takes, a slight twitch of her foot, a warmth that streams through her body. She wipes her fingers on her dress, rises from the stool, and draws the curtain in front of Folkví's bed before tiptoeing across the floor and opening the door. The clear air of evening. She breathes in deeply, fills her lungs. Rolls her shoulders a couple of times and stretches her neck, first to one side, then the other. Pillars of smoke rise from the houses around the yard. The sky is evening blue, some ducks arrow noisily over the treetops. Thora glances around, crouches behind the bushes on the eastern side of the house, pulling up her skirts and resting her elbows against her knees. Peeing, she picks up a thick, rotting stick from the ground in front of her, ants and beetles scatter. She shifts her feet so as not to pee on herself. How they scurry, busy little creatures.

As if it was part of a plan for her, Folkví is sucked backward into sleep's darkness with a squelch. In her dream her heel itches unbearably, she pulls off her shoe and scratches, her fingernails claw away skin. But scratching doesn't help, her heel swells, throbbing red and hot. Now she has a dagger in her hand, and balancing with her ankle on the thigh of her opposite leg she scores a deep cross. The outer skin is hard to penetrate, she must apply pressure to the blade, but once it's through it slices her foot open without resistance. She draws the knife back and forth a few times before removing it and pulling aside the flaps of skin. The flesh is bloodless and pink, with tinges of purple and milky membranes, almost like slaughtered fowl but she has no time to savor it because there, deep inside the heel, in the midst of all its pure, pliable flesh, a bright green bud protrudes. Resolutely she presses her thumb and forefinger into the open wound and grips the bud. Under it, her nails grasp a hidden sprig, and cautiously, so as not to pinch the bud from it, she wriggles and turns her hand, a tickling sensation spreads through her lower leg. As she pulls, a long seamless movement, the sprig emerges from her foot. Fat and muscle cling to it, and with the tips of her fingers she teases the threads free and they snap back into her heel. She continues the work, meticulous and unflinching, wriggling and pulling, stripping the sprig of foreign matter, until a sizable length protrudes from her. The more that emerges, the thicker it becomes, until it is a branch, and after a time she understands. The branch is endless. The thought ought to exhaust her, but the opposite is true.

When she wakes, the dream-vision is inside her. She sits up in the bed. It's been a long time since she last rose from it, but now she picks up a shawl that lies at the foot, throws it around her shoulders, and pulls open the curtain. The open room looms toward her, overwhelming at first, then everything falls into place, the room is large and quiet. She holds on to the wall to steady herself as she puts her weight on her legs. A band of pain shoots across the small of her back, her knees will hardly bend. She looks around. The light of the summer night comes down through the smoke hole above the fire and illuminates the gray embers, the gray and brown sheepskins on the floor, obscuring the rest of the room, blurring its contours. Two thoughts coincide: the moon must be shining very brightly tonight, and here she has lived always. The song of a bird sets off the stillness, and for the first time since Áslakr's betrothal she feels the tension in her stomach ease. It's only life. All the fuss, the anxiety and grief, it belongs to life and life alone. Its commotion is the strange unrest of living people, she is worn out with sadness. Everything is about to change. She sinks gently to her knees in front of the fire, draws up her sark, pulls the sheepskin around her bony legs. The living, and that which was living. When she is tired like this, she belongs to both. She tosses another log onto the embers and blows, the coals glow with her every breath. Flakes of ash flutter into the air. She follows their movement into the darkness, senses a trembling behind her eyes. The night bird's song is shrill in the humming silence, it draws her with it, her head drops forward abruptly. She sinks inside herself and turns to face the vision. And this time the branch pricks its way out of her heel without help, without needing to be cut free: it is more like a child moving on its own under the skin of the abdomen, looking for a way out, the flesh bulging until it is penetrated, and the green bud appears. Vigorous and scratchy, the branch grows swiftly from her heel, pulling with it tendons and flesh, muscles drawn taut, then torn. New shoots sprout forth, branches emerge, faster now, and at last a whole tree burgeons from her foot. In a moment it is taller than her and still it grows, propelled by its own will it thrusts toward the sky and reverses the balance of power between them. Folkví sees herself hanging upside down in the air, the tips of her hair dipping into the surface of the sea, sucking up water into her scalp, into her skull, her body and legs, and finally her foot, where the tree is rooted, bigger and stronger it grows, with buds that open into leaves, snapping brilliant green into blue sky.

Folkví completely forgets what she is waiting for and is about to get to her feet and go back to bed, it's not quite morning yet. Everything is spinning. But then she remembers that Áslakr and Od are coming to collect her today. She smiles at the thought of the surprise that awaits them, she being the surprise. A wave of excitement washes through her: *I'll dream now that this is the beginning.*

Three short knocks, a flutter of nervous expectancy in her chest. A stooping figure appears in the doorway, Od, good man that he is, standing in the light he lets in. A breeze rustles the pines outside, and their sound enters too, with the scents of summer. And behind Od she sees Áslakr, staring into the room, Folkví, he blurts out, startled by the sight of her seated there on the floor. Yes, she says briskly. I'm recovered now. She gets to her feet and goes to greet them. Áslakr places a hand on her arm as she kisses his cheek. In the yard behind them, in the early sunlight, she sees the helping-woman standing beside a horse-drawn cart, her back turned. Just a moment, she says, and leaves the two men, strides across the yard, and touches the woman's shoulder. The gray face turns toward her, soft and expressionless at first, its features then assembling in a look of surprise, lips parted, as if she was about to speak. Folkví looks at her and takes her hand between her own in greeting. Your help won't be needed after all, she says, I won't be going to the pasture. But come inside so that we can pay you.

She has handed them each a cup of milk and stands now with her buttocks against the table edge. Skål, she says, and raises her cup, Áslakr shakes his head, skål, Folkví, and they bring their cups together, Od likewise, Áslakr laughs uneasily. As she drinks, she glances sideways at him, her gaze strong. To hold on to someone at whatever cost, to want to possess them. As if it were your only purpose in life. She thinks too that it may well come to be.

Turning her back to them gathered by the table, she savors the situation, closing her eyes for a moment. Behind the dancing yellow-red flecks she sees her hair fan out, floating on the swell of the sea. She turns to face the others again. How long is it until the wedding? Áslakr is immersed in his thoughts, he doesn't answer, and she asks him again. The wedding, Áslakr, how long until the wedding? He straightens up, and replies distractedly, er, it starts in a week.

Were You Sleeping?

SPRING

A re you there? a clear voice sounds through the air from the other side of the house. Folkví clasps a hand to her mouth, it's Áslakr, he's home, she breathes. She looks at Od with wide eyes, he drops the ax to the ground and runs a hand through his hair. The light is crimson in the late afternoon. For a brief second everything stands still, and then she jumps to her feet from the tree stump she's been sitting on. She dashes around the side of the house, and there she sees him, Áslakr, standing outside the door, tapping his feet, looking about, slender, unkempt, and very strong, and then he sees her and his face lights up in a smile. She runs to throw her arms around him. Steps back and looks at him without releasing him. You're back! Look at you . . . you look so . . . you haven't changed at all, she says, blinking back a tear, and embraces him again, presses her chest to him. Áslakr cups a hand around her head, he's always looked after her, and she feels joy welling up from deep inside. His safe arms. The same old Áslakr, home now from the expedition. She notices something, a big lump of amber in a leather thong around his neck, light and expensive and very beautiful, she pulls back enough to turn it in her hands. It's tear-shaped, clear yellow with tinges of darker orange, a milk-white point. She taps a fingernail against it, holds it to her cheek and smiles. You're a strange one, says Áslakr, and Folkví bats his stomach. Why? she says. Why am I strange? He'd arrived with a pack slung over his shoulder, and had dropped it when she came running, now he bends down and starts to undo its thick leather straps, fingers fumbling, he's brought something back for her. No, wait, says Folkví, not yet. Come with me. There's someone you should meet.

She drags him round behind the house. The chopping of Od's ax has sounded out, crisp and clear in the still afternoon, now he drives it into the block and steps toward Áslakr with his hand outstretched. Od, he says as the two of them shake. Hello, says Áslakr. Áslakr. Yes, so I guessed. Od glances from Folkví to Áslakr and back again, it's

true what they say, you look like each other. A silence falls
between them. Folkví's cheeks are red from the fresh air,
she looks up at the sky, then from one man to the other.
When did you get back? she asks. We sailed in a couple of
hours ago. Áslakr looks tired all of a sudden as he answers,
he leans back against the woodpile. But you'd have heard,
surely? I was quite surprised you weren't there, on the
shore, but Folkví cuts in, I couldn't bear it, she says. If you
knew how many times I've stood and waited down there,
whenever it's been rumored you were on your way, only
it was never you, always the wrong ship, her gesticulating
makes a drama of it, and Áslakr smiles, how many times
was that? She lifts her gaze and looks him in the eye. Two,
she says. Two, you say, ah-hah. I'll remember that the
next time you swear it'll be the death of you when I leave
on an expedition, Áslakr laughs. But it will, says Folkví,
won't it, Od? Od, who has been staring into the air, looks
at her on hearing his name, shrugs. I think maybe I've
chopped enough firewood for today. Why don't we go in?
But Áslakr would rather stay outside, he's longed for the
light of Frøsted, and Folkví laughs and shoves him play-
fully. You're getting to be just like Father, you know?

As Od goes inside to fetch some blankets, Áslakr

kneels to light a fire. He looks at his sister, his eyes asking, who is he, what's the story? But she waves his questions away with a hand. You said you'd brought me something back with you? Oh, yes. Áslakr gets to his feet and goes to the pack he's dumped on the woodpile, undoes the straps, and pulls out a parcel, an irregular shape, wrapped in coarse linen. Here, he says, careful with it. They're all the way from the Sæterland. Folkví beams, her hands barely able to wait as she sits there cross-legged with the parcel in her lap, turning it over. A present for me, who'd have thought, she says, holding it up to the sunlight, as if she could see through it. Áslakr crouches in front of her, who indeed, he says. There's only two, though, I didn't know . . . Folkví unfolds the cloth and claps her hands together. Oh, but they're exquisite! A pair of funnel-shaped drinking glasses, she picks one up to examine it. The glass is thick and green, with little bubbles of air in it, a rounded lip, clustered beads of glass forming a pattern on its surface. Look what I got, Folkví shouts out to Od, who is just then emerging from the house with the wine, look! She holds the glasses in the air, one in each hand. We'll have to share them, that's all.

While Áslakr talks, Folkví looks at his freckles, listens to the deep tones of his voice. She studies his facial expressions and lingers on his lips. His fair hair. Áslakr laughs and blinks his eyes as he speaks, throws out his hand the same way their father used to, he's in a good mood. Effusive. He's fallen for someone, somehow she hadn't imagined it could happen. But there he sits, on the tree stump right in front of her, and Od pours more wine and looks at him, engrossed, as if he were really something, Áslakr, with his rough voice, going on about trivialities. The little green glass tips this way and that between his fingers in the sunlight. Now he frowns and gazes into the fire, as if looking through it, while his mind turns to matters more important than sitting here, and Folkví feels like laughing in his face, a single ha! loud and abrupt, doesn't he know how pretentious he looks? He's nothing but a big child, his beard's still sparse and soft, he's been on an expedition and has come home, like so many other young men, so what, and now he sits here with an incurable world-weariness. Earlier, when Od told him about his journeys around Sjælland, Áslakr stared at him in concentration as he spoke, putting in the occasional uh-huh. *Uh-huh* and *mm*. It's something she's only ever seen their father or the headman do, this way of letting your inferiors know you're listening. *You don't say.* The superior man's subtle encouragement, and she'd felt the urge even then to interrupt him, what kind of overblown scene was this they were performing: two men of different social standing engaged in weighty conference. Argh. But then Áslakr came out with it before she had the chance to take the wind out of their sails. Suddenly, without preface or preamble, it popped out of him, I've fallen for a girl, and Folkví just sat there in silence. A week earlier, shortly before their return to Frøsted, they'd stopped off at Ripa to sell some wares at the big marketplace there, and in the bewildering crowds of people Áslakr's gaze had settled on a young woman. Gerd. She's so very beautiful, Áslakr says, for the fourth time, and Folkví is exasperated. She's so very beautiful, he says again, and he tells them that at one point she raised her arms above her head, and at once a brightness lit up the land as far as they could see. You must have seen it here too? Od thinks he has some recollection of it, was it this last Sun-Day, in the evening? He was having trouble putting up a tent when there was this incredibly bright light in the sky, he'd looked up and blinked at it a couple of times, then it was gone, but there was a moment when he'd barely been able to tell the sky from the earth, so bright it had been. Folkví hadn't noticed anything. Most likely she was asleep, she thinks. Asleep? says Áslakr with disappointment, but it was quite amazing! As if Gerd at that moment took charge of the world, in the very instant he laid eyes on her.

Folkví closes her eyes and turns her face to the low sun. The wine has made her drowsy and defiant. She imagines holding her brother's face between her hands, tracing the line of his jaw with a finger, his high cheekbones, the strong ridge of his nose, imagines dissolving into that face, its ancestry, and herself. It's all the same anyway, him finding someone, when she herself is fond of Od, even if she knows it can't last. And over at the headman's house a few nights before the expedition, Áslakr had kept so close to her all the time, no matter where she went, she'd sensed something through the alcohol and felt the desire to show herself off. They carried on talking, she couldn't concentrate. He led her then, his little finger and ring finger curled around hers, over the empty yard in front of the headman's house, the cobbles glistened in the rain, her hair blew into her face. He led her into the hird house and without a word between them they climbed the ladder to the small loft. She didn't look at him, but hitched her dress up around her waist. He pulled off her undergarments and stroked her thighs with his slender hands. Then, he pulled down his pants and slipped a hand under each of her buttocks. Áslakr, she said. He smoothed her hair away from her face, his hand on her brow. Afterward they returned to the others, Folkví had laughed and chattered loudly, it was late, and several people came to talk to her. Now and then her eyes caught Áslakr's as he sat, elbows planted on the table, immersed in conversation with Bú. He looked at her then as only lovers do, and she was elated and reeled with love all night and in the days that followed.

An insect crawls on the back of Folkví's hand, she blinks her eyes, shakes it off. Away with you. Od strokes

her back. Are you tired? She leans her head against him.
It's getting cold. The sun has gone down behind the horizon, the light now slowly diminishing. Their talk has
gone on, Áslakr is showing them his forearm, the hit he
took, he tells them about how they defended a coastal
town. The agreements they made as a result. Folkví pulls
the blanket tighter around herself. Beside her, Od nods,
what were they like? he asks. Are they a threat? and Áslakr
must think about it for a moment. Yes, they are. But good
tradesmen too. Od nods again. Yes. Just as I thought. As
they speak, Folkví stares at her brother as if at a stranger.
His light-colored eyes, his fair hair in front of his face. His
strong, dignified features. And the amber gleaming at the
neck of his tunic. A grown man, she thinks. That's what
he wants to be, to sit here and talk about trade. Where did
you get that amber? she asks him. Áslakr looks up. I traded
something for it at Ripa. And again, an urge to hit him
rises from the pit of her stomach, she smiles at him and
says, I'm surprised your taste is so ordinary, and Áslakr
looks at her perplexed. Maybe that got to him. She stands
up and puts her hands on Od's shoulders. I need to stretch
my legs, she says. She puts her foot down hard on the
ground and turns it to get rid of an itch under her heel.

But there's a welcoming party in the hall, Áslakr calls after her as she walks away.

Under the yarrow that grows beneath the fence surrounding the yard, Folkví finds a good stone. She picks it up and wipes it on her dress, and with her thumb rubs away the stubborn soil that remains. Then she extends her arm behind her, as far as she can, and hurls the stone out over the field. It's still a fine evening, as its colors seep into twilight.

The stone strikes an anthill on the other side of a low fence and is brought to a standstill. She bends down and ties her dress up around her waist, looks out across the fields. The new grain sways gently in the wind. She stands there looking at it for some time, unmoving, deep in thought.

A time will come when Folkví irrevocably will be a young woman no more. It's hard to grasp, for there are moments, entire evenings sometimes, that refuse to end, when she seems almost to be trapped in frozen time.

When suddenly she decides to go back to Áslakr and Od, she breaks into a run, afraid they'll be gone by the time she returns. Not until she reaches the headman's yard does she slow into a walk, short of breath and bristling with an alertness that makes every impression stick. Some wizened white flowers border the foot of the house in the blue darkness, an occasional bird still sings, her bare feet in the grass now wet with dew, and there, as she rounds the side of the house, her hand following the wall, sit Áslakr and Od, still at the fire, drinking and laughing. Áslakr rises when he sees her, his face made dramatic by the dark shadows the firelight casts.

The Book
of the Norns

Urd stands beneath the enormous ash and stares into the well before lowering the wooden pail. It dances a moment as it reaches the water's surface. She tugs on the rope, overturning the pail so that the water can enter. A trickle at first, then all at once, and the pail is drawn down with a sigh. She grips the hard rope tightly in her hands and heaves with all her strength. The rope creaks from the hoist.

The water glitters in the sun, cold and clear, gleaming too, and sacred, as with both arms around the pail she carries it to the tree and tips it at the trunk. Urd waters the tree. Its colossal roots rise and fall, drawn through the earth like giant stitches before plunging deep into the cold earth. She licks some water from her fingers, runs her hand through her hair in the trembling heat, scratches her neck. Whoever has no past has no fate, and she has no past.

Not wanting to return to the loom, she decides to take a break from her task. She sits back against the cracked and bumpy bark and gazes out upon the worlds. From the hill she can see across to Midgard, and shudders: the strange life of men. Their time is a peculiar one: they are born, they grow up, grow old, and die. First it's spring, and they fall out with one another, then comes the harvest, a cry is carried away on the wind, and someone departs. Then another will stand with a warped smile, a sheepish look, all too much meaning attached to a simple exchange of words, a simple action. Urd has seen it, again and again.

To her right, a squirrel darts down the trunk. It stops in its tracks on discovering her, remaining motionless for a moment, a front leg held out in the air. She takes no notice of it, is quite as still herself, and with a sudden gathering of courage the animal scurries in an arc around her, continuing its route to the ground. No sooner has it set foot on the grass, where briefly it seems to take stock of the situation, than it turns back and darts upward again. Urd chews off a corner of her little fingernail, spits it out, and gets to her feet. She must return to the work. With the back of her hand she touches her warm cheek, tries to cool down.

On the other side of the ash her sisters sit silently weaving. Skuld looks up as she comes toward them and opens her mouth as if to speak, but closes it again. When Urd sits down, they continue their work. They have faces, and yet not, features as vague as masks. It's hard to tell if they are young or old, but their eyes are dark and oddly deep. They penetrate time. Needles are threaded, threads are cut. Blank concentration. Their eyes are shafts.

Everything is a dull hum of converging sounds: insects, the sun, the scratching of stiff fabric. The insects dance in the dry air, come closer and then away again, swallows dip to the grass, now and then a breeze passes through the treetop with a rustle of leaves. The tapestry stretches almost into infinity behind the loom. The sun is in the middle of the sky. The sisters' brows are moist with sweat.

Verdandi is the slightest of them, she tilts her head and with her shoulder brushes a lock of hair from her cheek. Gives a gentle shake of her head and blinks her eyes back into focus. A cat curls at the foot of the loom and she bends down, smooths the fur underneath its belly, and the cat shapes itself to her hand, arching its back with a purr. She locks her fingers together and stretches her arms, palms facing outward, away from her body. A creaking of finger joints. She yawns. Oh, well, she says, and closes her eyes to the sun for a short moment, shuts the loom from her mind, her shoulders dropping. Then she lowers her head, a slight stiffness in her neck, and picks up her work where she stopped. Skuld rocks lightly, backward and forward on her stool, a breezy, tuneless whistle emitting from her lips. She weaves in the colors as she will, between the warp threads Urd draws taut.

Folkví's thread has long since been cut. Her life was strange and short. Now the sisters grapple with Áslakr's, as the world approaches its end, when it will sink into the sea. The coming of Ragnarok will be portended to men by a great Winter, three years long, with no summer in between. A blizzard will blow from all sides, they will be unable to go out and will see nothing through the frenzied storm. They will stumble and fall and get to their feet again, and will not remember how silence sounds. Everyone will starve. Nothing on earth will have the benefit of the sun, for it will warm no more. And then, after three long and desolate years, with every household isolated, the sky will break open, two wolves will swallow the sun and moon, and the world will be plunged into the sea. Even the gods will die—

Before a new world then rises from the waters. This is how it is, all mankind knows it to be so. One day winter will come. Urd thinks of it, and yet doesn't. She blows a lock of hair from her brow and looks out across the landscape. At the horizon, Midgard.

The Book
of Áslakr

Confused Dreams

A sound disappears, dwindles away. Áslakr must have been half awake without realizing, because he opens his eyes the moment it's gone and listens intently. What was it? The room is completely still. All night his thoughts have circled on the betrothal, on Folkví and Gerd, Ranva. A nightmarish exchange of roles, first it's his sister handing him something and then turning away in a rage, now it's his daughter. But the odd silence displaces it all into the background, it's toward the silence that everything inside him now inclines as he opens the curtain around his bed and steps into a pair of felt shoes, his joints snapping. Nothing can be heard but his breathing and the voices of the birds outside. He runs a hand across his chin . . . Bird voices . . . Not a wind to buffet the roof or howl in the nooks, and no rain to lash the side of the house. No cold either, to scuttle across the floor and cling to his calves with fingers long and thin. The silence echoes in his head, the absence of the storm that has raged since the winter, and as if afraid to waken the weather once more he goes through the room almost on his tiptoes. He leans into the front door, its hinges squeal as it opens, and in falls the light, golden and clear. Already there's a warmth in the air, the like of which he hasn't known in more than a year, all of a sudden it's pleasant, like a morning in summer. But this is mid-autumn.

The headman's yard is awash with great puddles. They lie stagnant about the muddy, gray-brown enclosure, mirroring the sunrise, the lilac sky. It all looks unreal. A pungent smell of leaves and earth after endless months of rain. And while everyone else still sleeps, he stands there, he alone with the birds, in the midst of the altered landscape. He pulls off his felt shoes and rolls up his night pants before stepping out from the shelter of the overhanging roof, out onto the sodden earth. Into the warm light. His feet sink, the mud is cold and smooth, the warmth of the air a strange contrast, and although the birds are singing, they serve only to highlight the backdrop of silence. He crouches down and leans over a puddle. At first he's startled, it's been a long time since he saw himself so clearly. His hair is streaked with gray, darkly mottled, and the furrows in his face have grown deep, like gouges in wood. His nose appears to have grown bigger, more prominent, as his cheeks and eye sockets have become sunken. But the lines are the same, the jaw and the straight ridge of the nose, the wide inclines of the cheekbones. His eyes are narrow. He draws back his lips and checks his teeth. Both rows are intact at the front, straight and yellow-white, none as yet hideously black, he runs his tongue over them. Turning his head, he considers himself from another angle. Not bad at all, could be worse. He looks like his father. And Folkví. And maybe it's the confused dreams he had dreamed in the night, or maybe it's because he's crouched here admiring himself like a woman, that what comes into his mind is the day of his wedding, when they found her drowned in the fjord. It wells up through all the years and is suddenly near again. It was the hottest day of the year. Folkví's long hair fanning like seaweed, wafting softly just beneath the surface. Only her face above water. He and Od had to drag her ashore.

A movement makes him look up. On a mound a bit further away, a group of rabbits have emerged from their burrows. They hop away from one another in different directions, their bodies elongating, bedraggled and starving after the dreadful summer, but boisterous now too, as playful as youngsters. On a tuft of limp, yellow-green grass, a blackbird stamps the soil in an effort to lure to the surface an earthworm or two. Still crouching, Áslakr lifts his face to the sky, rests his forearms against his knees. The warmth is a mask. From behind the house he hears the clucking of the hens. He is cold inside, still cold even as he moves, but slowly the warmth enters his skin, seeps into his body, and the pressure in his chest gradually lifts. His skin feels tight across his nose and cheeks, this is hardly to be grasped, is everything actually going to be all right? Was it all just a wretched half year? And then, the festivities this afternoon: a small contraction of his stomach. The sun has returned on the day of the big celebration. Today, Ranva is to be betrothed, and soon the hirdmen will depart on their winter expedition.

When shortly afterward he goes inside again, his long legs feel weak. Ranva, he says, pulling back the curtain in front of his daughter's bed and sitting down on the edge of the berth, Ranva, wake up. Ranva peers from blinking eyes before opening them abruptly. What, she says then, and turns to face the wall, closes her eyes again. I think it's over, he says. The weather. I think that's it. He smooths her forearm with his hand. You think so, says Ranva, with no tone of inquiry, and Áslakr senses immediately that he might as well give up. He'd hoped she would be enlivened by such good news, perhaps throw her arms around him, press her cheek to his chest, and in reply he would have held his hand against her back, for the worry is gone and he is her father. That's what he'd imagined. A cloud scuds across the sky, dragging its pool of

shadow along. It passes on. It was dark, but now it's clearing up, the problem is no longer a problem, and if it's only
briefly that a person can savor such relief before turning
back to his work and the daily round, at least there is a moment for joy, before everything becomes yet another story,
a joy that is for all, that is almost euphoric. Remember that
dreadful summer? We were so afraid it was the end of everything. What a terrible time it was. Or the ship disaster,
or the time the sheep died one after another, and it was the
wrath of the gods. He wants someone to share it with, and
he wants it to be her, his daughter, they are supposed to be
family. He looks down at her. Her eyes are still closed, but
he knows very well that she's awake and is shutting him
out. Exactly the way she did when she was a child and
someone came too close, grown-ups she didn't know, who
tried to make contact—so inapproachable she was, lying
there on her pillows in the dimly lit nook with her made-up
games—she would close her eyes then too, turn her face
away, other people weren't allowed into her world, it was
far too precious and fragile for that. Pretending to sleep
was her shield. But why resort to it now, at eighteen years
old, how come he so seldom can get through to her? Why
can't they be like father and daughter, bound wistfully on

this day of her betrothal? A bashful sort of pride clings to her and has made her never the easiest person on whom to bestow one's love, there's something inviolable about her, he thinks, it's as if his care for her offends her, like an observer she stands and looks on, wrinkling her mouth when he says something stupid, never abandoning herself to exuberance or impetuousness. Never allowing herself to get heated. When the other children played, she would mostly stand on the sidelines, her big child's head held high, arms at her sides, an indulgence in the way she looked at them, as if by watching them she was learning what mistakes she wanted to avoid. Other children would climb onto your lap, paw your face, they would mimic your facial gestures in a wordless form of conversation, but not Ranva, after the age of three she'd rarely offered him even a little hand to hold. It had only heightened his need to touch her, to pick her up, to be allowed to comfort her. The mere thought of everything she had to contend with on her own was enough to make his chest tighten, sometimes her detachment felt obsessive. Maybe it's because she never knew her mother, he thinks to himself, descending into despondency. I've tried to keep up and watch her grow, the way a woman watches her daughter, but she has never let me in.

There is a closeness we have never known. The crumpled newborn he lifted from Gerd's breast, the baby's cries intensifying then, piercing, stuttering cries discharging from her tiny body: her sobbing was frantic and inconsolable, he'd bounced at the knees to hush her, holding her close to his chest, the way he'd seen women do so many times. He shakes his head. How bleak that the dead should come to him so early in the morning. And today of all days. What are you here for? He looks down at Ranva. Gerd was only sixteen. The same age, more or less, as every woman who has left him, and like so many times before, he studies Ranva for traces of Gerd, the few aspects he thinks he remembers. But Ranva resembles his own kin, especially Folkví. From time to time his sister's features stand out so clearly in his daughter that for a moment he is quite bewildered, whereas Gerd, it would seem, simply vanished with her death: as if nothing of her remained behind.

His gaze has wandered now, he stares out into the room, eyes fixing emptily on a knot in the timber. The wood surrounding the knot is darker than the rest, sweeping upward in elongated circles. It looks like a man in a pointed hat. Áslakr sees faces all around, the man in the hat is watching him now as he turns toward Ranva again, noting how controlled her breathing sounds. She is most definitely awake. Her overt rejection lodges in his being as a despondency. His spine is hunched, his neck juts forward, but the little man's gaze prompts him to pull himself together, and so now he rises. I think that was it, yes, the bad weather, I mean, he says, and gives Ranva's shoulder a squeeze through the blanket, though with no response beyond a slight pause in her breathing. Through the open doorway he senses the brightness and warmth that have succeeded the wind. But he has no wish to leave her, it's hard to let go of something one soon will be forced to release. Even if she holds herself aloof and turns away, they are a unit, as long as they're still living under the same roof; her body is there, in the same spaces as his, he knows what she's doing, is familiar with her routines, there's an intimacy that goes with sharing a house. It's an intimacy even if she doesn't want it. He doesn't know what's going to be left when it's gone, feels a hard pain in his throat, the size of a child's clenched hand. And abruptly Ranva turns over to face him, she opens her eyes and looks straight at him, expressionless, or indifferent. She stares at him as if she doesn't know who he is, almost as if he were an object and not a man, and he stops in mid-movement, pausing like prey, not knowing what else to do. Her gaze lingers. Then, she sweeps the covers aside resolutely and angles past him as she goes through the long-room. Oh, yes. The weather *is* nice, she says a moment later from the open doorway.

He wakes from new half-dreams in which he is young: birds circle, screeching about the mast as the ship nears land, an awkward sense of disquiet among the crew. Ranva is standing there staring at him, and he straightens up, blinking, his neck painful and stiff, he must have fallen asleep where he sat, his head against the wall. Under her sark is a woman's body. Áslakr looks away. Runí's here, she says, her face and voice different now. She's animated and happy, but it's not meant for him. All right, he mumbles. Give me a moment and I'll be with you. But put some clothes on, you can't go outside in that. Ranva looks down at herself proudly. Why not? she says, and smiles at him, drawing energy from somewhere else, from something he has nothing to do with. He smiles back at her, abashed. You can't, that's all. Her eyes are lively now, they can be like that too. Of course I can, she says, and wags a finger at him, putting him in his place. Then she goes back out into the yard, and he hears their bright voices. They drift into the house on moist, warm air.

F rom the yard comes the sound of the hirdmen's song. They're boisterous, completely dazzled by the change in the weather, and even more so that it should coincide with the celebration of the betrothal and the impending winter expedition. Áslakr tries to shift his focus to something inside him. To observe oneself is a silent act. The shadows are short, the sky saturated now, dark blue, and beyond the fence the treetops rise, yellow and orange. As he stands there behind the house, bending over the tub to wash himself, the sun is almost unsettlingly warm. Through the open door he can see Ranva moving about, distant and concentrated as she picks things up, holds them for a while, and puts them back in place. But then he feels that the man in the timber-knot is watching him again, and obediently he moves his gaze to the hens, which have sought the shade of the house. They rest with their heads sunk down, as if the previous months of endless rain never existed for them.

The landscape holds a soundless rage, is the thought that comes to him. He wrings the cloth into a ball in his hands and tips his head back as a great flock of lapwings crosses the sky. Are they heading south . . . now? Not only is it a month later than usual, it's the first hot day all year. Today of all days, they think the cold is coming? He rubs the moist cloth over his chest, adding the migrating lapwings to an account he's been keeping of nature's signs. That he is unlikely ever to see them again, the lapwings, is something he won't think about now, but his hope has ebbed somewhat since this morning. He looks around him, drapes the cloth over a branch to dry, and stands with his hands on his hips. His skin tingles in the warmth, the hirdmen's song gathers in volume, and the injustice of it all can then no longer be ignored, because the headman has decided that Áslakr will no longer take part in the expeditions. And though it was formulated as a question, when he drew him aside to tell him, there was no doubt that it was intended as an order. In a way it's a release, Áslakr had told himself tentatively when afterward he

trudged home, whether it's this year or next, what difference does it make? He pulls on a pair of wide-legged trousers and wriggles into a clean tunic, the linen, bone-dry,
prickles his skin. But whichever way he looks at it, it's still
a lot to lose all at once, at the very least he'd have liked to
have known the last time that he was on his final expedition. You understand, don't you? he says to a hen that has
come out of the shade to peck about his feet, its feathers
caked with mud. I should have taken my chances when I
was still young. He glances involuntarily into the house,
but Ranva is nowhere to be seen. The hen, on the other
hand, looks at him keenly, its orange eye attentive and
offended at the same time, and yet in its own way it seems
to be listening, Áslakr thinks, and with that it all comes
welling up, his indignant sense of having been robbed of
something, a different future perhaps. Or a different past,
he corrects himself, but still: the chance that life might
have shaped itself differently if only he'd stayed over
there, which, in a backward kind of way, he thinks has
been taken from him. The expeditions have always glit-
tered and gleamed and drawn him back to the first aston-
ishing time he was away, they brought a lightness to his
being that remains in him even now. Whenever they ap-

proached foreign shores, he would sense the young man inside him. He looks toward the woods, the last of the lapwings disappears from sight over the crowns of the trees. It's past now.

Áslakr went on his first winter expedition when he was twenty-one years old, and back then it had felt as if the world was suggesting to him that life could be different entirely. It was early morning when they neared the Sæterland, the air was fresh and cool, and everything inside him was in turmoil, it thrust in his limbs, for the Sæterland too was a place in the world, even though he'd never been there before. The sensational feeling it gave would not leave him. His body swayed, his calves quivering as he stepped ashore. The men, almost a hundred in number, were ordered to remain in the harbor area, loud and high-spirited they strode off the ships, hands shielding their eyes as they gazed up the slopes: behind its fortifications, the town spread up the hillside. Everything was inconceivably green and steep. Áslakr's heart was pounding, and while the others stayed behind, he and the headman, with a small entourage, had ventured through the marketplace, which only then was beginning to wake. Sand-colored tents stood row upon row, they looked delicate in the dawning day, a wind wafted through them, he remembers the sound of gently flapping fabric and the thin blue sky with threads of trailing white. In a dip in the ground, a group of people were already gathered around a tub in which they were dyeing linen, they looked up with sleep-drenched faces, followed the men with their eyes. Áslakr straightened his shoulders and rejoiced: to this place he had arrived now, a stranger. It was a solid, substantial feeling that filled his chest.

On their way up to the king's yard, the headman strode with purpose and resolve, reflecting on the proposal they would put forward, nodding firm greetings at those whose gaze he happened to meet. Áslakr followed suit. The gravel lanes gleamed. The people of this strange town watched as they passed, and Áslakr's hand kept clutching at the knife in his belt. Every sound caused him to jump, his ears would not take in a word of the headman's instructions, but buzzed instead with his own commotion of thoughts. He tried to look earnest but couldn't. He looked at the stone houses and thought: What would it be like to grow up there, in that house? Or there, in that one? In a town so much richer, so much bigger, with new people arriving all the time? Who would be his sister there? A slender hand passed through the air, cleaving it in two. It belonged to a woman crouching at a stream, she sank her hand into the water while looking up, engrossed, at a woman who was talking to her. Her hair was careless, elegant. Or, another time, a man with wide-open eyes grabbed his arm, pointed toward the fells, speaking quickly to him in a hushed voice, and would not let go of Áslakr's tunic, only then to switch abruptly into a shrill laughter, his hands flapping the air in front of him before he backed away and was gone, leaving behind him a reek of urine. Áslakr laughed with some of the men, holding his stomach as they tried to mimic the foreign language, its rhythms and melodies, how strange it sounded. But soon it settled in him, he got used to it, and a gleeful satisfaction radiated inside him when in the midst of someone's babble he began to recognize an increasing number of words. When all of a sudden, turning a street corner, he realized: I can find my way on my own. It was a delight to engage with the new as if it were old and familiar.

One night a large fire burned on the shore, the hirdmen had blackened their eyes. In the warmth from the flames, they took off their tunics and caroused. We're at full gallop, he'd thought to himself, nothing can stop us.

Both rider and horse. The feeling strengthened in him, and he looked down at himself as the flames roared against the blue-black sky. Muscular arms and sturdy thighs, wasn't he a giant? This was a world for men. The smoke of a bonfire in clothes and hair, dishes of meat passed among them, he ate with his fingers, chewing the sinewy flesh soft in his mouth. He swallowed the last chunk and withdrew briefly from the company. The constraints of home had fallen away. With Folkví's gaze no longer upon him, there was no limit to who he could be. One who could hold his own among many, who could casually sharpen his sword as he sat in the camp and conversed with others. It was all so uncomplicated to him. No longer did he feel the need, under the constant, watchful eye of conscience, to think through his every action in all its consequences, brood on how a matter might turn out, review his every utterance. What would Folkví say and think? She would snort at him in the background. But a person can reach a point where all is before them and their gaze is fastened only on today, tomorrow, perhaps the day after. He sat down on a tree stump and started clapping the beat of a song some of the others had started, joining in with an unfettered howl, before grabbing the ankle of a servant girl and pulling her toward him . . . Waking the next morning, he was rested and content. The servant girl went past him among a small group, he sent her a smile and trotted up alongside Bú, lunging at him then, throwing an arm over his shoulder and tickling his stomach. Ahead of them a lapwing plunged, it was such a carefree day. He went around the foreign town with an effervescent ease, and people recognized him and lifted their hands in greeting.

We're Meant to Be Celebrating Here

So this is where you're hiding! Runí laughs, separating his syllables—ha! ha! ha!—and slaps a hand on Áslakr's shoulder. He is small in stature, with a broad, pleasing face, he looks like someone who just woke up, trusting and warm. His skin is golden, eyes green-brown with fine purple shadows underneath. He's very young, barely more than a boy, but his dark beard is thick and full. And Áslakr says, yes, yes, so it seems, though it's hard to see how it could be construed that he is hiding, standing alone as he is in the open yard under the sun. You disappeared so quickly after the betrothal, so I said to Ranva I'd go and see where you went, says Runí, guiding him, still with his hand on his shoulder, around the puddles, in the direction of a table around which people stand in clusters, smiling and laughing or engaged in serious conversation, hands gesticulating, heads tilting. In the midst of this animated scene, Áslakr's eyes find Ranva, who stands apart, a hand resting on the table behind her, her face turned away. She looks like what she is: someone who is waiting. Young and reserved, and as solemn as when Runí a little earlier placed the garland on her head to seal the betrothal. Áslakr, watching from the side, thought to himself, what happens, happens.

The dark blue robe makes Ranva look taller than usual, she looks incredible, standing there in profile, and she turns toward them then, hey, Father, she says as he comes within earshot. Folkví's face flickers in hers, and Áslakr is startled. She studies him a short moment, but smiles, pushes a wayward lock behind her ear, her throat held forward slightly, and Áslakr returns her greeting, hey, he says with a little smile, and Ranva takes hold of Runí, leans into him. Now they are at just the right distance. She is young and normal, Áslakr loves to see her like this, full of good feeling, alert. Runí, who is a bit shorter than her, kisses her cheek before filling Áslakr's glass to the brim, splashing the sides of the glass as he pours from the jug of cloudy, expensive wine. And Áslakr sips, rocks on his feet as Runí's stubby thumb moves up and down Ranva's waist, eager and yet restrained. She is physical, present. There is a soft and defenseless ease in her bearing that he has not seen before. She is such a person in honor of Runí, that's how it appears, as they stand there in front of him, that their bodies exist in each other's honor. That all the care and attention Áslakr has given her has been for this: that she may present herself to another family, that from his daughter's timid being steps this woman—that's how it is, Runí a boy, she a woman—who squints up at the sun now, such an ordinary thing to do, and yet Áslakr cannot look away.

Runí, who has been glancing around restlessly, turns toward Áslakr, ha! ha! ha! he bursts out again. He chinks his glass against Áslakr's and replenishes them both. Ranva straightens her shoulders and rolls her eyes, she looks bashfully at Áslakr, and Áslakr laps it up, skål, my young people, he says, looks them each in the eye in turn, almost brimming. In the background, the musicians have now tuned their instruments, they strike up a song, Runí wipes his mouth, says, shall we? Ranva looks at Áslakr, and everything sinks inside him, of course, says Áslakr, by all means, I can look after myself, he smiles at Ranva heroically and Runí gives his upper arm a dig, we'll find you later, he says, have a nice time, before leading Ranva away toward the chain dance. Áslakr follows them with his eyes for a moment, then gazes at the ground. Hm, he says out loud, studying his shoes, stretching his toes inside them. Moods are a strange thing. He drains his glass and walks a few steps with his hands behind his back. Hm, he says again.

He joins a festively clad group, nods a round of silent greeting, tastes the wine that is poured into his glass. Most of them are craftsmen and women from the town. Thora, who now runs her own household at one of Frøsted's farms, resumes a story she was telling before he appeared. So there he is, standing in the pouring rain, up to his ankles in dung, and I ask him if he needs a hand, she says. And then, she splutters, barely able to take a breath, then he looked me up and down, and said no. He said no: *thanks all the same*, she shrieks, and the company bursts into laughter. Thanks all the same, she gasps, tears running down her cheeks, and Áslakr drains his glass and joins in the mirth, though he has no idea what she's talking about. It doesn't matter. It's obvious it's funny, and what he wants is some fun.

The mood is unusually lively, a din of voices, cups

clacking together, I knew it, someone says, we've worked as hard as ever, of course the weather had to change. After the long rain, and the winter that encroached so far into summer with its cold and dismal days, the relief is palpable, everyone is looking their best. Áslakr has trimmed his beard so close his face looks bare. But his eyes gleam. He reaches for the jug on the table behind him and pours himself another. The sun is scorching. He's dripping with sweat. Beads of it dislodge from their points of origin and run down him, swift as a brush fire, no, that's not it, he backtracks, more like tiny babbling brooks, trickling down his body in unfamiliar routes, from his armpit down to his hip bone, for instance, or from the back of his knee to his ankle. My body, Áslakr thinks, and swigs the wine, smiling, my body is an entire landscape, and now a rivulet penetrates into the thick vegetation of his groin. The lowlands, yes . . . I am terrain. He ponders this for a moment, for it's a good thought. He is an environment for something, the way the headman's yard in which he stands is his own environment, the way the fjord and the woods and the steep banks before the shore are his environment too. But what then is the environment's environment? He looks around at the friendly faces and breathes in, draws in the air to feed the fluttering sphere beneath his ribs. Who commands the world of men? Is it the Æsir, are some of them really so big that a man is to them like a drop of water? He feels a warmth in his stomach. The mood he's in, everything looms so large all of a sudden, his thoughts run away with him, nervous hands that sketch out pictures in the air: a glimpse is all he gets before it's gone.

Talk has turned to a thyle from the neighboring district, somewhat younger than Áslakr and rather popular in the Østland, who came the previous week to predict the weather for them. Thora looks at Áslakr. What did you make of him? Everyone directs their attention to him. Áslakr takes a swig of wine, flaps his hand in front of his mouth while he swallows. Not a lot. I helped him home, he says with a snigger. I didn't mind, it was no problem. His audience laughs. Unfortunately, there was only room for him in the back of the cart. More laughter, louder now. I had the headman with me, you see. Important matters to discuss . . . life, and the like. Ha ha ha. Someone has to. I'm afraid I couldn't quite catch what he was saying in the back there. I mean, it was pouring down. They laugh again, though a bit surprised, and

Áslakr laughs even more. But then the headman's wife, Trude, steps forward, she clears her throat and folds her arms across her chest as if now, in this light and high-spirited atmosphere, to say something serious. Since you were so kind as to send my guest home a day early, she says, what do *you* have to say about the coming winter? What's it going to be like? What omens have you read? And everyone falls silent, their laughter peters out. Áslakr tries to concentrate while Trude expounds on her concerns, his eyes fixed on her face, its dark and trustworthy cast, the focused energy she projects, uh-huh, he says now and again as she holds forth, not listening to what she's saying, simply observing her. It's almost too focused, he thinks. Everything about her, the frown that crumples her brow, the deep tone of her voice, her eyes and their dog-like sadness. The alcohol courses through him. What's she standing there for anyway, stirring up worries, we're meant to be celebrating here, and he looks at her critically, she's plump, and getting on a bit too, is there something she's angling for, something she . . . wants? Is that what she's up to? The headman's Trude, is she making a *play* for him? If she is, she's picked the wrong person, he says to himself, people often assume that just because he can be quiet and serious sometimes, *can* be, it means he prefers the same in others. But that's not the way it is at all, not in the slightest, no. Not in the slightest! Ha ha. She's got another thing coming, if that's it. Not on your life, Trude. If that's what she's after.

Now Thora pipes up again, she mentions a dream she had, very bleak and frightening, and Trude's unfortunate outcome of a daughter joins in too, expressing her general feeling that something's still not right. Some listen, stroking their chins, others grumble their concerns. Áslakr looks at them. He frowns and follows their talk with his eyes, as if it were a torch passed around among them, his gaze dwelling on the speakers' mouths, lips, incomplete rows of teeth. A bit of bubbling spit. An old man chomps revoltingly as he says his piece, his words deliberate and slow, he has difficulty pronouncing them, and breaks off with an *alas*. Alas, Áslakr repeats to himself, and something rushes inside him, cloaking the meaning of all words. He sways a bit. Then he drains his glass, wipes the corner of his mouth.

A young woman has come up alongside him, now she grips his sleeve and tugs on it. She rubs the fabric between her fingers, runs her thumb across the golden embroidery at the cuff. How special it is, she says softly. He looks down at her. His eyes struggle at first to focus on something so close. Red curls. A daughter of Runí's cousin, he remembers. He saw her last a couple of summers ago when she was still just a gangly girl, tottering about like a calf, wobbly and shy, now all of a sudden she's this bold creature with a pretty face . . . out of the child's pleasant neutral features a woman's face has emerged, with dark, close-set eyes and a finely arching nose. He smiles at her and reaches for the jug, the wine spills over as he pours. It's a gift from a woman, Áslakr whispers, and holds a finger to his lips. He's about to say more, searches for the words, wanting to pinch the young woman's cheek, to feel her firm flesh, when Trude says his name. With some hesitation he straightens his shoulders and turns his face toward her. She looks at him in annoyance, and at the young woman too, far too young in her eyes, how close they stand together, but she will not abandon her errand. In other words, she says, have you taken note of anything? And at first he just looks at her, but then her words seem to repeat themselves in his mind. He nods, barely a movement.

Since Folkví's death people have come to him for

omens, but his abilities aren't nearly as clear-cut as hers. What he has is *knowledge* of nature, and this year nature has been hard to gauge, without any discernible order. The lapwings deciding to migrate now, for instance, as if a hard winter lies ahead, whereas the fleece of the sheep is not yet thick and coarse. Which would indicate the opposite, if it wasn't for . . . what? If it wasn't for everything being so completely unknowable. Without precedent. The anomalies are endless, never in his experience has nature been so at odds with itself, but of course he says nothing of this. He swallows a mouthful of wine. Worst of all is the tree down at Folkví's old offering site: there it stands, among autumn's yellowing, half-bare trees, its branches bearing bright green buds, only now on the verge of opening into leaf. And then there are the visions, they appear to him suddenly, overpowering him in the midst of his daily routine. Snow everywhere, a mantle of snow thicker than any he has ever seen. He clears his throat and looks Trude in the eye, no, he says, I'm getting old. I've read no omens. But it'll be a mild winter, I imagine, and he throws out his hand, almost striking the young woman in the eye, why wouldn't it be? Gentle days follow months

situation he's put her in, left hanging after asking him for his considered opinion, an answer, between the two of them, two people of the same high standing in the town, even if at the end of the day she's of higher standing than him, but here he is brushing her off, and so she must have his attention, his respect, and says to him now: Well? Joking aside, Áslakr, answer me that. What do you know? But Áslakr isn't even paying attention to her, he's turned to the young woman. He scans the yard quickly, Ranva is nowhere in sight. It's incredible how some things never change.

And then Áslakr decides to sing. His outgoingness is a thin veneer, his voice reedy and tentative, and as Trude makes herself scarce, so seething with rage that she could cry, the people around him fall quiet. They look at the ground so as not to deter him, not to unsettle the vulnerable face he wears tonight. Áslakr feels his heart in his chest. This strange, living creature that conceals itself behind his ribs, which he has seen so many times in slaughtered beasts, pumping in the snow. He thinks of a horse, the stomach split open, a pair of big hands clawing out the innards: the dark liver, the blue-tinged guts steaming in the cold air, and there, the great, complicated heart.

Pumping and pumping, like a flapping fish on land, pulsing on with dignity but without sense, as the snow around is spattered red. The image melts away, rises through his head, and vanishes, the world is around him now. His pulse strikes up a beat, and he follows. He sings, brighter and louder. The wine is at work in him. He turns his face to the sky to hit the high final note. Then he opens his eyes and feels the gaze of the young woman once more upon him.

Later, he leads her to the stable. He cups his hands around her buttocks, and in that moment he is a young man again: his life is ahead of him, only it isn't.

Unknown Wife

A vague sense of the night before coalesces slowly into an image of the young woman with her back to him. He sits up abruptly. The girl's face turns toward him, deliriously contorted in a brief glimpse. His headache radiates out into every part of his body. But that was all, wasn't it? Nothing more? He leans back into the bedding again, dissecting the celebration piece by piece as it comes back to him: Afterward, they'd glided over to the hall, the girl clinging to him a bit, he'd leaned back against a pillar, and when she kept prattling on, tilting her head to one side, fidgeting with an earlobe, he'd walked away from her, wondering where her parents were, her brothers, uncles, cousins, why didn't they stop her from humiliating herself? She stared at him, insecure and sorrowful, that was the look she gave him as he sat down at the long-table and fell into conversation with the other men. But he quickly found himself bored, too many stupefied, ruddy faces, the conversation slow and never venturing beyond the boundaries of politeness, until eventually it died out and they leaned back, smiling vacantly at one another. One man picked at a fingernail before lifting his gaze again: Anyway. It's getting late. Áslakr craned his neck in search of Ranva, but she was still nowhere to be seen, had gone home, he was told, and then he remembers jumping to his feet impulsively: Runí better keep his hands to himself, and Bú, guiding him back to the bench. Sit down, he told him gruffly. Áslakr had tried to get up again, but Bú's strong arm held him in place, and then a fatigue had come over him, he retreated inside himself and sipped the ale that was in front of him, he feels nausea rise up in him at the recollection. He'd sat there with sunken shoulders, inclining his head toward whoever happened to be speaking, laughing every now and then. Áslakr is mortified. In another glimpse he sees Runí smiling at him, Áslakr is trying to tell him something about Ranva, and Runí squints, his eyes have laughter in them, he finds Áslakr ridiculous, Áslakr says to him, you think you're pretty smart, huh, Runí pats him on the shoulder and says, enough now. Áslakr wrenches his hand away, lay off me. Hm, says Runí, why don't you go home and get some sleep, Áslakr. His eyes are laughing more than any mouth. And Áslakr swats the air dismissively, pfft, and puts on a smile, a hideous grimace. Don't think you're so clever! he hisses, and smiles his not-a-smile.

I'm a wolf, he thought to himself shortly afterward, when he saw Runí cup his hand to his brother's ear and whisper something, they emanated strength and youth, and their glances were cast in his direction, hurh hurh hurh, Áslakr heard Runí's brother laugh. How little it takes to offend boring people. Haven't they ever seen anyone who can drink before, haven't they ever seen *anything*? And yet they've both been on expeditions. I'm a wolf, he thought again, beware me when I wake, and he growled then, or grumbled, and his eyes closed, he listened to the oscillating sounds of the room, a clamor of chinking glasses, chatter, stomping feet, and laughter. A chill ran through his body from his hands and feet, a sweat broke out, beading from navel to forehead, delivering with it a sharp dizziness, and he staggered out, pitched forward, clutching at those he passed to keep his balance, and all his body could say was *home*. Emerging into the dark night, he threw up outside the hall, someone placed a flat hand on his back and said his name, did that person follow him home? Didn't she take the key chain from around his neck and let him in, put him to bed? He sees the girl's face in his mind's eye, how he reached out to her and stroked her cheek as she sat on the edge of the bed with wide, earnest eyes, and now he sits up again, abruptly, his fingers fumbling at his chest for the key. It's still there. So he hasn't lost anything. He lies down on his side, arms together, lies with open mouth, and his heart beats fast against the straw.

Dried vomit is stuck to his hair, he picks it out, then gets up. The movement makes his head thump inside his skull, but he can't stay in bed any longer, he needs to greet the day. His thoughts won't leave him alone. In the long-room he acknowledges the thralls in a voice that is deep and rough, they nod in return and carry on their work. He's not the worst person they could serve, he thinks with a measure of satisfaction when one of them places a bowl of porridge in front of him at the table with a look that mostly seems indifferent. The stodgy substance makes his stomach knot and he closes his eyes, listens to a hum inside himself, slumber descends on him, interrupted by a thought: It's hard to imagine the headman despairing of

himself after a night like that. But then again, the headman does not split into two. He isn't one person in the
daytime and another when he drinks. He is the same calm
authority. He'll sing, certainly, and laugh long and exu-
berantly, and even be silly too, he can engage whole-
heartedly in conversation with those in his company, and
yet he's never really anyone but the person he is. He'll stand
there the next day, feet planted firmly apart out in the yard,
the warrior commander's staunch stance, he will laugh
from the pit of his stomach and say something funny
about the night before, but he will never have anything to
feel ashamed about. There's no weakness to him, nothing
unchecked that might reveal a pitiful side of him, he is
simply more of a man. Áslakr debases himself when he
drinks. Now he remembers rounding on Rúní, telling him
there's something he'd got completely wrong, something
he'd gotten wrong right from the start, and the moment
comes into focus, more details return: He'd stepped up
close to Rúní, his chest puffed out, arms held back as he
spat out the words, those around them went quiet and
still, alert to this sudden flaring of temper, and Rúní's
eyes were not laughing then, but still he didn't lose his composure. He put his face into Áslakr's, whispered between

his teeth, his breath warm and sour, you're embarrassing yourself, then stepped back and walked away, turning his head once to the side to send a gob of spit to the floor, before joining his brothers. One of them put an arm around Runí's shoulders, they came together in a cluster like they were a gang of kids, and Áslakr let himself be riled by it, what kind of behavior is that? Why do the young people have to display their sympathies so physically? Girls leaping to their feet to give comfort, a team-like indignation when one of them is unfairly treated, boys draping their arms around one another. And at the same time they seem to think they're so grown up, they send their protective, indignant daggers out into the room around them, presumptuous little pretenders not worth engaging with, oblivious to the fact that real grown-ups would never act like that. You don't see older women close ranks around one of their own who happens to feel unjustly treated, soothing and consoling, you don't see them tuck their hair behind their ears and discreetly survey the room, hoping that they will be observed in their solicitude, in their strong attachment to the group.

After Runí retreated like that into his pack, Áslakr stepped first in one direction, then another, his chest still thrust out, glaring at them through narrow eyes. Well? he shouted. Well? But they slipped back into the throng, the hubbub of voices returned, and after a short time he sat down again on the bench, sensing the sidelong glances that came his way. He looked around, but no one would return his gaze. And so the only thing to do was stare at the glass in front of him, raise it to his lips, and sit on his own. He tried to break into a conversation between Trude and Bú, there's something Runí doesn't know, he muttered, leaning toward them with a crooked smile. He's deranged! They looked at him briefly, then carried on talking, pretending they were immersed. Bú! Áslakr tried again, prodding Bú's shoulder. Bú was his friend, and belonged to the hird. There won't be any expedition this year, you just don't know it yet, he almost shouted, but Bú simply turned to him in irritation and said: No one's listening to you.

Áslakr squirms, all is misery. He turns his spoon slowly in his porridge, then pushes the plate away. He gets to his feet. Where's Ranva? he says, to no one in particular. A thrall looks up and points toward Ranva's berth. Good, Áslakr thinks. Good, good. So she hasn't spoken to Runí yet. Tell her I'm at the hird house.

Outside, the sky is light, white almost, not at all the discordant blue of yesterday. More like it should be in autumn, not that it comforts him particularly, it's still so strangely hot. The air doesn't seem to reach the lungs. He gasps for breath a couple of times and goes behind the house, where the hens strut about on their spindly legs, still a bit lethargic, but at least they've bothered to get up today. They look nervous, as if they don't quite trust the earth underfoot, and only with caution stretch their frightfully long toes toward it, clucking softly. The one from yesterday has curled up a leg and stands poised for a moment without noticing him, suspended in an impossible balancing act. Their small heads tilt from side to side, their staring eyes peer, they behave as if they're old and frightened, communicating in their anxious, secretive language.

A pitiful cockerel, hatched during the rains, bedraggled and runty, weak-looking, stands motionless at the edge of a puddle and looks up at Áslakr, the eye that's turned toward him blinking as he approaches. How inconvenient to have eyes on the sides of your head, he thinks, and bends down quickly, snatching it up by the legs. The cockerel puffs itself up, its feathers raised, it shrieks, and he slams it hard against the side of the house. A spasm runs through its body, then it is still. To make sure, he grips its neck and pulls the head back until it snaps. The hens cackle and scatter. He tosses them a handful of grain and hides the dead cockerel under his cloak before crossing the yard, his eyes fixed on the ground ahead of him. He isn't up to being confronted with what happened last night. Some figures are making straight toward him, he glances up quickly to ascertain who, but it's no one, just thralls, and he clutches the cockerel's legs, the other hand holds his cloak closed over it.

It was on one of that summer's gray and stormy days that Áslakr discovered the beech tree down at Folkví's old offering site. He'd been out to see how much damage the rains had been doing along the fjord when suddenly it was there in front of him, beckoning in all its wrongness.

Among deep-green trees whose great crowns were sway-
ing in the wind, this one was bare and young, with small,
hard buds. The water was high, rain whipped into his
face, and somehow just then he didn't think further about
the tree, it was only that evening when he lay in his bed,
agitated with boredom, staring out into the rushing blue
darkness, that his mind returned to it: Had he really seen
it there? How could he have been so oblivious? It couldn't
be real, surely? A sudden burst of spring in late summer.
Early the next morning, before anyone else was up, he
battled back through the rain to the offering site, he
needed to know if he'd imagined it.

When he again saw the beech tree with its small
smooth buds on the verge of opening, while the other
trees would soon be submitting to autumn, he sat down
on a rock by the fjord and could only imagine that it was
Folkví, who after all these years was making herself
known to him in order to tell him something, for the tree
was connected to her. It grew on her offering site, and it
was there that she had drowned. What do you want,
Folkví? he'd mumbled, only half in earnest, he'd never
been in touch with the dead. The fjord was dark and turbulent, the wind crashed through the trees around him,

but apart from that nothing much occurred, and he was just about to get to his feet when his vision was disturbed by a fleeting image, he saw the woods covered in a waist-high layer of snow. All the contours of the landscape were obliterated, the world was transformed into great white shapes against a dull white sky. He shuddered and drew his cloak closer around him. What was this? An omen of Ragnarok? He prodded the wet earth with a stick, feeling oddly unmoved, he could have gotten up and gone back to the yard, brow against the cold rain, but he forced himself to stay put. He really wanted to go home. So this is the lay of the land . . . Is this where it all ends? He felt like shouting at the top of his lungs. Farewell, world, was that it? The wind howled in his ears, his thoughts wandered, he had to concentrate to keep them centered on the approaching end of days as other matters announced themselves vociferously, a chanting ensemble inside him, his feet tapping the ground to its beat. Churning, senseless thoughts, like whether the rain was dancing on the fjord and pricking holes in it, yes, that was exactly what it was doing, it was pricking holes. The winter lay ahead like a threat. And I am like the winter, old and immense. Somewhere in all the noise was a criticism too, he thought he ought to be reacting differently, certainly more strongly. What did it say about him, that he was unable to collect himself? But then Ranva appeared to him in his mind, and he gave a start, three quick contractions of his guts, and all the turbulent energy suddenly concentrated into a single point: Ranva's life was not over, not by a long way. This creature, essentially a mystery to him, who grew and behaved in the most surprising of ways, so unlike him . . . behind the grief he felt at her independence lay a vague hope. He looked up into the crown of the tree. The buds almost trembled against the gray-black sky! Was it not as if the beech was drawing nourishment from the living world around it—that it was almost *sucking* the sap and the life from the surrounding trees to feed itself? Soon the other trees would fade and wither, while the beech would unfold into leaf. Ranva should be the one to share in that, it had to be her, she was and always had been strong, a life that could consume the lives of others. That was apparent even as Gerd died giving birth to her, he just hadn't realized it, not properly, not until now. She's an immediate replacement, he thought, almost made to take over as soon as others let go. She will be the one to endure, to see everything around her come to an end and be destroyed, while she herself will live on. The next thread in the tapestry will have a whole new color, that was what he told himself as he laid out a plan for Ranva's survival instead of his own, with hardly a sense of sacrifice.

In an old story he and Folkví had been told when they were children, two people would survive Ragnarok by living in the woods. Áslakr turned it over in his mind: In a way, it made sense. Wouldn't there be a place, somewhere between Midgard and Utgard, that might be spared the great Winter, as the clash between the gods and their enemies raged elsewhere? He had begun to build a house for Ranva and Runí beside the tree that very day, for no matter how much it bothered him, Ranva would have need of Runí to carry on the family line. Áslakr himself would end his life in the raging blizzards, most likely succumbing in a bank of snow, his mouth and nose filling with ice until he could no longer breathe. By then he would have lost all feeling in his arms and legs, and would have had plenty of time to realize that this was it as his body slowly shut down, chamber by chamber. Tears came to his eyes, it was like plotting an act of revenge against himself, and then he felled two birch trees and fashioned four corner posts. The wood was fresh and wet, it wasn't good, but it would have to do. Behind the beech tree, at a suitable distance from the fjord, he laid the foundation of a house, reasoning that the patch of woods most likely to survive the winter would be there by the leafing tree. Here, life would sprout, while all else died in the snow.

Outside the gate, Áslakr follows the path awhile in the direction of the village before veering away and walking over the hills toward the fjord. Now that there's no one around to wonder why he might be carrying a dead cockerel with him, he turns his cloak over his arm and flaps his shirt for air. A light breeze passes through the grass, and for a moment he pauses on a rise and looks at the view. The fjord lies in front of him, a metallic base to the landscape, stretching coldly into the distance. There's something shifty about it, as if it could expand and approach at anytime. He knows how deep it is, the walls of the basin dropping steeply away from the shore, but from where he stands it seems hard and stable, an open tract of land that may know no end, and he tries to picture what it will look like after the great Winter, when the world sinks into the sea. He imagines that the little spot in the woods where the tree and the house stand will still be there, an island of flourishing green in a ceaseless expanse. He turns and looks toward the headman's yard and the yellowed trampled paths that extend from it, the age-old routes of those who have lived there. To the left, the cows, their muzzles in the soggy grass. Their movements are peaceful, barely there: a lazy swish of the tail, the twitch of an ear. He sets off again, his knees absorbing his descent down the slope. The cockerel dangles from his fist.

It does him good to be out in the fresh air, forcing his body into motion. It puts things in perspective. Inside the house, he is tormented by self-reproach, behind the curtain of his bed it consumes him completely, but here, set against the hills, the sky, the tall trees, even the cows, it dwindles into inconsequence, evaporates. It's nothing. No matter, he says out loud, and is startled by his voice. A time-tested protest clears his conscience further: It wasn't just me. Everyone was at it. People were all over each other, their mouths open, hands groping under clothes. No doubt there were fights too, women weeping out of old jealousies, a couple of people passed out where they sat. No one remembers all the details, he can relax, he's just an ordinary man in an ordinary life. His behavior, too much to drink on the occasion of giving his daughter away to be married, will be forgotten in a day or two, will become at most an anecdote at which he'll wince while the company has a laugh about it, he'll even chime in, ha ha, no, not my finest moment, ha, and wait for it to pass. Yet this train of thought too grinds to a halt, it makes him angry that he might be such an object of mirth, humiliated, that he should have to shake his head jovially at his supposed shortcomings when it's Runí, who isn't half his worth, who they should be laughing at. He's a dolt, he has no idea the things I do, Áslakr says in a low voice, and kicks his heel against the trunk of a fallen tree. He has reached the fjord now and goes toward the offering site, where the vegetation is thicker, pathless. Thorny undergrowth clutches at his trouser legs, resolutely he forges his way, holding back low-hanging branches, pressing through the thicket. A pair of birds take flight as the branches swipe back and close behind him. His way becomes clearer, the terrain opens out among the trees, large swathes are waterlogged, the earth is a sodden mass of dark brown and rotting leaves from which birch trees rise, pale and tall. A warm white light penetrates through the treetops, and there, ahead of him, he sees the beech tree, the house behind it. As ever, he is surprised at the sight. But with each day that passes, his surprise diminishes and becomes more predictable, like looking at his finger and moving a knife toward it, anticipating the incision. Yes, it's still there. Today the leaves of the beech have unfolded completely from their buds and they flutter, new and velvety, incandescently green, in the yellow woods. He puts down his cloak and the cockerel on a stack of logs and pinches a shoot from a twig, rolls it between his fingers, until the smell of fresh leaf rises to his nostrils. He flicks the little pellet into the water. The cockerel's head hangs limply from the woodpile.

With a hand propped against the trunk, he considers the house. It's odd to see a house in the middle of the woods. Impossible, almost. He feels an urge to erect a fence around it, a ring of protection. It's not very big, more like a pit house, a single small room with a sleeping berth, a fireplace, and room too, if luck is with Runí and Ranva, for a sheep. But each stick and branch that has been woven between its posts, in and out, behind and in front, the next layer reversed, to form the wattle, is his own work.

Every detail is his own conception, his own fashioning, not that he didn't know he was capable, but to think that he's actually done it. The accomplishment, as distinct from mere possibility, he thinks to himself with some pride. Out here, possibility is mostly behind him, everything that never came to anything, everything that never will. Now he looks at the house and knows that he has built it. He will keep the daub in a tub, and while he's patient with finishing the wattle, for everything has to be thorough and precise, he is eager to complete the work, to seal the walls and finish the house. Rather unconventionally, he has already placed the roofing beams and overlaid them with planks, giving the most important element priority in the way he structures the project.

The ideas mill in his mind when he is at work here, he wants to put down a floor and daub the inside walls, make a chest, if there's time. It's impossible to know, the snows could come tomorrow. Yes, why shouldn't they, it could happen today for all he knows, though it is hard to imagine in the warm and grainy air. He goes over to the heap of cut branches he uses for the wattle, and as he picks them apart he feels a pressure behind his eyes. He is happy out here. There's a simplicity about building a house that he has not known for many years, it brings a lump to his throat. Here, his actions are easy, as if occurring of their own will. He picks up the ax and hews some planks without thinking about it, as he has need of them. He stands still awhile and calculates how much he'll require, before immersing himself in the task again. He sweats, pulls off his shirt, wipes his brow with it, and tosses it on top of the peat-stack. The days have passed, while the woods around him have slowly withered. While the beech tree has opened out its leaves. Now all that remains is to complete the front wall, he'll be finished today, and then the Winter can come.

He wishes Gerd could see him now, what he is doing for their daughter. Or is it just something he tells himself out of obligation, for when he thinks about it he can't imagine Gerd any older than when he knew her. Their daughter . . . It doesn't sound right, he's used to thinking of Ranva as his alone, and has difficulty grasping that the fifteen-, sixteen-year-old girl he was once married to could be her mother. The thought that Gerd could have been with him now, plumper, with creases in her face, he knows he would have loved her, at least he thinks he would, but he just can't see her in his mind's eye. His thirty-four-year-old wife. He sees her most clearly as she was in the days they first met, their days together at Ripa, the town where she grew up, he recalls how overcome he felt, that everything happened so suddenly and unexpectedly, from one day to the next there she was. It's a forbidden thought, that they might have shared the time since then, quiet talks about their daughter in the evenings, an ordinary daily life, wind gusting through the smoke hole above the fire. Gerd as a confident, competent housewife, children of various ages clinging to her skirts, held rapt by her face as she cards wool. His thoughts want to continue along this path, but he reminds himself that such figments too belong to the realm of possibility, to that which never transpired, and aren't worth concerning himself with anymore. He stretches his back, a pop of his spine, then turns to a new pile of branches. It ended the way it ended, he tells himself, though the beginning was good indeed.

On the way home from his first expedition, they put in at Ripa for a few days to trade some wares before the final leg home to Frøsted. Áslakr had felt grown-up and strong, but ready too for homecoming, the weeks at sea had made him look forward to seeing his sister again, returning to the familiar house of their parents. That first evening at Ripa he had gone about on his own, had strolled through the marketplace with his hands behind his back, a new habit he'd acquired, without thinking of anything in particular, wandering at will, absorbing what he saw. The language was once more their own, and soon they'd be home. Over by the fence his eye was caught by a small group in the dusk, he nodded an acknowledgment, it was a couple of men from the hird along with three others. He wandered on, wishing to remain awhile in his own wordless silence, to feel the months in the Sæterland settle in him, but then something drew him back, and without surprise at his decision he turned and joined them. Why not spend time with the others now and savor what was left, their high-spirited fatigue? Bú and Holger, hirdmen both, were laughing and joking with two young men and a woman from the town, their faces smooth and sleek in the rough dimness. The young woman was standing apart from the others, as if not really belonging in the company, or perhaps more as if she did but wasn't sure she wanted to. Áslakr glanced sideways at her while listening to Bú and Holger: the landscape, the weapons, the food, and, most amazing of all, the local methods, and Áslakr nodded meaningfully, until his cheek felt distinctly defined, for wasn't she looking at him now? He cast a glance in her direction, and immediately she looked away, her gaze drifting from one thing to another, and then she stretched, thrusting back her shoulders and arms in an odd twist. It was all rather affected, he noted with great satisfaction, she was trying to look relaxed, and not very successfully, but the thought had barely formed in his mind before he forgot about it, because then she stretched one arm as high as she could and the sky lit up, as if from below, out at the horizon. In a slow, rolling movement, the heavy clouds became a white luminescence in the darkness. The others looked around in surprise. Soundless thunder! Something significant was surely going to happen. But Áslakr already knew what it was.

The next day they sat facing each other on a bench outside the magnate's residence. An ash tree swayed above them as curious younger siblings and cousins peeped from the doorway, only to be yanked back inside by the strict hands of servants. Whenever anyone passed by as they sat there under the tree, the pair would lower their heads and gaze at the ground. Áslakr smiled at Gerd. She propped herself up on one arm as she sat in the mild spring air, which was warm as skin. Her father had looked him over carefully when, a couple of hours before, clean-scrubbed and with his pulse racing, he'd stood before him and asked permission to talk with Gerd. And now there she sat, next to him, without speaking. He was a good match. Her thumb stroked her wrist, and he didn't know what to say, he had been so excited and so certain in his attempt that he hadn't given a thought to what they might do when they were together. So here they sat. He thought: Her lowered gaze, why does she make such a secret of her eyes, it's not making things easier. She fidgeted constantly, her whole hand now moving up and down her bare arm. And her eyes, like a swirling abyss—at last she lifted her head and looked straight at him. It was as if her silence concealed a mystery . . . there was something buried in her! He wanted to bring it out. He heard himself begin to talk, in the stillness she left for him to fill, and with her gaze upon him now, it wasn't exactly agreeable, it was overwhelming, and overly serious. But they couldn't just sit there quietly looking about, that would be too strange, and afterward, what would she think, and what about her family? What did he have to say for himself, the young man? Nothing much. Oh, but he must have said something? No, nothing at all. We just sat on a bench. And so he began to speak, tentatively at first, episodes from his growing up, I've hardly any family and my parents are dead, he said. He blurted it out, and then stopped again, the way she was looking at him made him feel self-conscious and strange. He wondered if he was making her uneasy by isolating her in such a way, putting her there beside him, perhaps she was discomfited by the whole situation, or perhaps the opposite, maybe she was very much in control of the situation, superior to him, his utterance hanging in the air between them. She was shy and intense. How are you feeling? he asked her then, and a smile suggested itself on the wide lips that shaded into the hue of her face. Good, she said, and so they sat there with their bodies turned toward each other. He laughed, though not too loudly, and felt at once both glad and serious, that's good, he said, and thought as hard as he could. Every beginning sounded wrong, but knowing he had to start somewhere he began with his sister, with Folkví, he only had the one, no other sisters or brothers. She would have to meet her, he said, but the thought occurred to him the moment he suggested it: Could any two people be more different? Folkví, the nonstop talker, and this girl beside me, Gerd, so bashful. Folkví, so quick to judge and to lash out. Gerd barely says a word. And even as he thought these thoughts, he carried on talking, as if to argue against the notion, and said: You might find her a bit hard to handle, a bit excitable, but once she gets to know you she'll accept you, even if she does sometimes come on a bit, well, out of the ordinary, I suppose. Gerd looked away, was it the wind that moistened her eyes? He had no idea what was going through her. She tossed her head, parted her lips, closed them again. Then she looked at him, holding her breath: I love to weave, were the words that tumbled out. She gathered herself, as if to venture something more. It's hard to explain. But it's the sitting on my own, working away at it. A lot of people find it dull, but I like it, you have to be focused and precise. I could sit like that for hours, days even, if no one interrupted. She smiled faintly. And Áslakr felt something leap in his chest, what did she weave, what motifs? Now he felt truly happy. He sensed an uncomplicated levelheadedness in whatever she did. Her voice was soft and restrained, she seemed to be a person who considered her sentences carefully, he leaned forward to listen to what she said. It depends, she said. At the moment, I'm weaving a tapestry with my sisters. Perhaps you'd like to see it later on? They looked at each other and beamed, everything in a whirl.

When the last of the goods were loaded on board a few days later, they sat beside each other on the shore and she made him a gift of a piece of amber to hang around his neck, it was her own. Each morning he'd stood and waited for her outside the house, as slowly and surely she erased every thought of other possible futures. She was probing and withdrawn by turns. She didn't pour herself out to him, but listened and spoke, and guarded something too, her eyes still a void. Is there something desolate about her? he wondered, strangely uplifted by the thought, while the waves rushed against the coast. He took her hand, so delicate and warm, she lifted her face. I'll be back soon, he promised, to arrange the betrothal with your father.

That was what has taken root: the days between them, as they sit on the shore. She picks up a handful of sand and lets it run through her fingers, they sit apart from the others, near-silent, faces turned to the sea. He puts his arm around her, and what they proceed toward overshadows everything, it's simple. He doesn't know her.

I Hope You'll Be Happy

Áslakr steps back. It's barely to be believed, but he's ready to daub the wattle. Although he hopes that it'll be a while yet, or supposes he does, he glows at the thought of the day when the blizzards will hit, how Runí will thank him sheepishly from the bottom of his heart when Áslakr tells them about the house. For while everyone else will flock together and begin to help or oppose one another in their efforts to stand against the insurmountable Winter, Ranva and Runí will pack a few things and retreat into the woods after a brief farewell. Ranva will step close to him, and the duration of her embrace, the look in her eyes, will say all there is to be said. She and Runí will be able to say goodbye only to Áslakr, otherwise there'll be a scramble for the house. It must be a secret between the three of them, and they'll stand for a moment in front of him, young and bewildered yet strong, and Áslakr will follow them to the gate and watch them as they vanish into the whirling snow, an almost rosy-gray glimmer in the air. And just as the snow closes around them and their figures blur, Ranva turns, the features of her kin shine on him, but Áslakr smiles and waves his hands to indicate that they must be on their way.

A rumble rises in his stomach. It's too early to roast the cockerel, so he munches an apple instead. If he lights the fire now, the coals will be ready by the time he finishes the daubing and he'll be able to blood-spatter the house. He tosses the apple core among the birch trees and starts to build the fire, he keeps a small supply of kindling inside the house. He bends down and picks up a pair of plank-ends he's left by the end wall. Pauses in midmovement. Is that cockerel watching him? He sets down the kindling carefully on the ground and looks up at the dead fowl on top of the woodpile. It's lying completely still, or did its chest just rise and fall then? The head hangs down side-ways, the eye he can see is wide open. As the eyes of hens and cockerels always are, he tells himself as he straightens up, putting his apprehension to rest. The pale, foggy light over the fjord makes the pupil gleam white, it seems to follow him as he steps away to the side. But it's only a reflection. The fjord and its surroundings, just being out here in the middle of the woods, all those thoughts of Ragnarok have got him imagining things. He wipes his hands on his trousers and goes to pick up the bird. He lifts the little head gingerly between two fingers, it's light and limp, and a sound escapes him. He turns it over to examine it from the other side. Not that such an eye ever tends to suggest intelligence, but these are definitely extinguished. Flat and empty, as he is accustomed to recognizing in the dead. Still, he might as well chop off the head while he's at it, and he looks around for the ax until a new idea occurs to him and he sets a heavy log down on top of the cockerel instead. A flattened fowl, not such a pretty sight, and an unpleasant crunch is heard as the skeleton gives way under the weight. Now, at least, it will stay put. He brings the tub of daub to the wattled wall. The air is still close and warm.

Death can occur in so many ways. Sometimes it's as if life simply seeps away very slowly. A person seemingly dead may still be among us. Or someone alive strangely absent. He rubs his tickling nose with the back of his hand before plunging both fists into the daub and slapping it onto the wall, half an eye looking out over the fjord as he works. Its waters are frozen and covered with snow, a hard wind sweeps across it. Snow whips through the air. Áslakr blinks a few times, stands quite still and waits for the vision to recede, the fjord to return to its normal state, peaceful, insects humming above the surface. But perhaps he should work a bit faster now, he thinks, then remembers the fire he had begun building. Has he taken leave of his senses today, or is it the hangover? He starts doing one thing, only to abandon it halfway through and start on something else. This accords poorly with the meticulous approach he wishes to apply to his work here in the woods, and now he gathers up the heap of kindling he forgot about earlier and carries it to the fire site with the sense that he is tidying up after someone else. As he builds the fire, Folkví keeps appearing in his mind. To what higher authority she made her offerings is something he's never been bold enough to hazard a guess at, but certainly she had not seemed like a person who'd found peace. The emptiness that usually defines the dead had not manifested itself in her corpse . . . She'd looked so *frightened*.

Yes. He remembered how she exuded it, as if there was still unrest in that cold, stiff body when they hauled it onto the shore.

It was Od who saw her first, when Áslakr and he, on the third day of the wedding, had gone out to look for her. No one had spoken to her since the evening before, but still Áslakr was not overly concerned, everything was panning out for him the way it was supposed to. He was young. The sun was shining. But as they made their way along the path toward the offering site from their parent's burial mound, Od had suddenly shrieked and dropped to his knees, a madness upon him, and without knowing what was happening, Áslakr was consumed by fear, the day turning metallic and pale around him. His heart pounded, his eyes cast about. He saw in staggered flashes, his voice clawed its way out of his mouth, as if across an obstacle, as when in the grip of a nightmare you are unable to issue a sound until startled awake to your own piercing, bestial scream. What is it, Od? he cried, shrieking himself as his eyes followed the line of Od's gaze, into the fjord, and there, among the reeds, he saw her: her face bobbing in the cold water, her body and hair floating just below.

When some four or five hours earlier the headman's yard began to wake, everything had seemed so peaceful. He had lain in his bed behind the curtain, listening to the small sounds of birds, carts, thralls beginning the day's work, but also to what was less usual: people clearing their throats and coughing, murmuring voices. These were the guests, beginning to stir. Gerd was not in the bed beside him when he reached out for her with a weary arm, already used to her presence. Befuddled after two days of drinking, he got to his feet, his body aching from nights without sleep, and staggered through the long-room, where relatives from distant places lay slumbering on the benches. He supposed that Gerd had simply gone off on her own somewhere, the last couple of days had been a lot to absorb, and she was only fifteen. Her body felt so small underneath his. He could scarcely believe his own joy, having this moment alone to take stock of it, and he only hoped that Gerd felt the same way. Perhaps she'd gone down to the fjord, and immediately he felt the urge to go and find her, to stride out after her, light-spirited and purposeful, he wanted to know what she was looking at, the water surely still as a pond today. The warmth on her body if she sat quite still, the cool morning breeze a kind of undercurrent. He realized that he was in the midst of it all now. A shudder went down his spine, he imagined her silent, for to him she was more a state of mind than a train of thought. At the first wedding feast a couple of days before, she had sat wordless at his side, absorbed in him, her hand under the table moving up his thigh until it cupped, light and quivering, his groin. Her daring, and the fierce will it seemed to reveal, made him freeze. Shifting his loins with a sudden forward movement, he glanced quickly at the others seated in their vicinity, his gaze coming to rest on her face, which was turned a little away. Her round cheeks, the slight bend of her neck, the darkness under her hood when she turned her head and looked at him. He would take care of her, yet his desire was huge and heavy, without tenderness. She had sent him a smile that was at once shy and self-confident.

Out in the yard, he was greeted cheerfully by those he met. Balls and sticks from yesterday's games lay abandoned in the baking sun, the day was unusually hot, even though it was still early. He washed his face in cool wellwater and took several gulping mouthfuls before going over to a group of men who had gathered in the shade of the headman's house. Their faces were dopey and soft-looking from too little sleep and too much alcohol, their clothing grubbier than when they'd arrived. The mood among them was slack and lethargic, a throaty laugh issuing here and there as they tried without success to balance two sticks on top of each other. Morning, said his cousin Olav, who had come from the far north. Life treating you all right? The others nodded to him, energized by his joining them, an opportunity to tell again their stories about the night before. Áslakr sat down with them in the shade, declining with a wave of his hand when one of them extended a jug of ale. His body trembled with fatigue. He waggled a forefinger vigorously in his ear as if to kindle his thoughts. This really was his wedding. The atmosphere was good, and the most important guests had received extravagant gifts upon their arrival. Everything was as it was meant to be. Even Folkví had been behaving fairly normally, considering the madness of the summer, she'd kept her distance and only once or twice taken him aside and looked him deep in the eye, and he had embraced her then before extricating himself and returning to the festivities. I hope you'll be happy, she whispered, and he replied loudly, yes, yes, brutally ignoring the cloying sentimentality with which she was trying to keep hold of him, his guilty conscience. He rubbed his eyes. Fortunately there was Od, this reliable transitional figure of hers, a fine man. She'd get over it, and with time everything would be normal again, she would find a suitable husband of her own standing, they would have children. Áslakr's and Folkví's children would be cousins who would grow into strong youths as they themselves would weaken and age. It would happen gradually. Up until now, life had progressed slowly, there'd been so much to see and do, but now time would tip, it would run quicker, like a peaceful afternoon it would suddenly be gone, their mother had said something along those lines to him on her deathbed. When everything falls into place, time will *slide*. Wasn't that how she'd put it? And although at the time it had sounded dreadful, what, an afternoon? he seemed to understand it now, he could actually relish the thought of putting his childhood behind him once and for all and living a quiet life as Gerd's husband, if he only knew where she'd got to. Has anyone seen my wife this morning? he asked the group of men, and Olav seized the opportunity to poke fun, so, Áslakr, now it starts, he said with a laugh. If I'm not mistaken, I saw her sneak into the headman's. But no one had in fact seen her, and before long Áslakr accepted the jug of ale, the thralls began to put out the herring and the porridge on the long-tables inside the hall, and the sun rose higher in the sky. He was rather drunk by the time Gerd leaned over him and put her arms around him from behind, pressing her moist lips to his cheek, and he turned halfway toward her, surprised at her spontaneity. Gerd, so there you are, he slurred, tilting his head against her thigh. And look how fine you are! He got to his feet and held her out in front of him with outstretched arms: in fresh, clean clothes. Have you been at the fjord? She smiled rather oddly, and during the meal, as they sat at the table, she laid her head on his shoulder. Through the alcohol, he registered sharply that something was amiss, where did such behavior come from all of a sudden? He felt like shaking her off. Her father stared at her admonishingly from the other end of the table, he'd put down his spoon and sat with his hands placed heavily on the table edge, though she seemed not to notice. Her eyes were closed. Áslakr gave her a nudge and she shook her head and straightened up, as if coming to her senses. There was something off. She looked too young and submissive. But when tears welled in her eyes at his irritation, his sense of her shifted again, for she looked like a small animal too, she looked like a guilty child, she looked like someone bewildered at having done something wrong, and his annoyance turned to pity. It doesn't matter, he said. We just can't sit like that, that's all, not here, not at the table. You must sit up straight like a respectable person. During the rest of the meal she observed him in a way that was newly alert, attentive to his every movement. He finished his food, sucked some fat from his thumb, then looked over at her and met her gaze, and he felt despair, for he sensed a resistance, like a thin, shivering finger that traced the length of his spine. What was going on with her? His smile was worried and stiff.

After the meal, he removed himself and hurried from the hall before she could come with him. He joined a couple of friends and spoke conspicuously with them, leaving her on her own, urged by a furious momentum to distance himself from her. He wanted away from the clinging tentacles of women: What if it had all been too hasty? Take a step back, and all intimacy was at once repulsive, no, what he wanted was only to be himself again, in the company of the hird, and the desire to drink came upon him anew. Across the yard, he spotted Od ambling idly around, as if at a loss, until he saw Áslakr among the swarm and came straight toward him. Congratulations, Od said, and before Áslakr could answer, he asked if he'd seen Folkví anywhere. I can't actually remember having seen her today, said Áslakr, looking about. I'm not even sure she was at the meal just now. He grabbed hold of Trude, who happened to be passing at the same moment. Have you seen Folkví? he asked. Trude stopped and chewed her lip. Uh-uh. Not recently, the last I saw of her was yesterday, I think. Hm, said Áslakr, and let her go, then said to Od: She's been on her best behavior all through the wedding. But we know she does go off on her own sometimes. Od nodded. In fact, said Áslakr, we could go out and look for her, I've a good idea where she'll be. Od seemed relieved. My imagination's been running riot, he said, I woke up from such an unhappy dream last night. Áslakr lifted his hair from his sweaty neck to let the air reach his skin. Let me just alert the one who's in charge of the afternoon's games, I'll be right with you.

On their way through the woods he could feel how good it was to get away from it all for a short time, he was already excited about seeing Gerd again. It was wrong of him to be so harsh on her, what was the matter with him?

The awkward mood between them was something that needed to be put right: as soon as they got back he would go to her and hold her tightly, whisper an apology of some kind and some reassurance. He quickened his step, it needed to be resolved. The friction had to be dispelled, surmounted by good-natured and unambiguous actions. He tried to imagine how she must be feeling but could not put himself in her place, instead he thought about all sorts of little things she did, for example the way she ate her food in a busy, squirrelly way that was at odds with her usual poise, the way she covered her mouth with her hand as she chewed. She's shy, he thought with satisfaction, it was one of the things he liked about her. His thoughts turned to his unstable sister, he stared into the neck of Od in front of him and felt anger. That they should have to go out in the woods, during his wedding, that he should be pulled away from Gerd to look for her, she who had ruined his period of betrothal with her moist eyes and unintelligible murmurings. Her helpless demands on him, all the summer nights when he had lain awake, prickling with rage that she could take command of his thoughts with the entirety of her weakened being. He had thought it would never cease, that he would never come free, and he had dreamed about her, that she was an old, whimpering dog he kicked in the belly. His foot went right through, dust whirled up, for the dog was rotten and stank.

They had almost reached his parents' burial mound, where Folkví would sit so often, but even from a distance he could see she wasn't there. They approached anyway, standing apart and looking around. The woods were peaceful. Od turned to him. Where can she be, I wonder? Well, said Áslakr, and scuffed at the soil with the toe of his shoe. Let's go past the offering site at the fjord on our way back, and if she isn't there, she'll be in the hall when we return.

The flames rise, curiously transparent in the afternoon light. The fjord laps the shore. For a moment, Áslakr gazes into the fire and anticipates with pleasure the dusk, the birch trees that will stand out so clearly, the shimmering water, and the wind that will begin to pick up as the sun descends. The roasted cockerel he will pull apart with his hands and devour after protecting the house with its blood. The air is strangely misty, a foggy membrane stretched across the sky, allowing him to look directly at the sun. No no no, he breathes as he sits and considers the peculiar white disk that hangs above the fjord. The whole sky is a pale yellow blur, the fjord beneath it a yellow sheen. He shakes his head. This muggy weather, the water reflects into his face, he feels so tired now. His hangover is worse, he looks at the beech tree a little further away, the shadow of its crown in the gritty light. He won't be breaking any agreement if he sleeps for a bit. When he wakes, the day will still be long. He gets to his feet, takes his cloak with him to the beech tree and spreads it over himself like a blanket, rests his head against his forearm. The birdsong seems loud all of a sudden, the shadows of the tree move across his face, he lets fatigue wash over him. A gentle breeze, the sounds of the water and the trees, the deep cooing of a pigeon, and out over the fjord Folkví's suspended face, her face is shimmering in the air. His eyes open and close. Now they walk together, side by side, feet in heavy sand, they come to the crest of a hill and are met by a hard and blinding sun. It's very simple, he is a brother. They sit down in front of the house they grew up in and make plans for the following day, Folkví's voice is gay. There is a force that streams out into the world. The pale grass and the warmth in the air, their expectant chatter. He blinks his eyes. The fjord glitters before him.

On their way home from that first expedition, before the ship put in at Ripa and Áslakr met Gerd, in the middle of one of those long days when, unsheltered from the rain, he was securing the sail and shouting something through the wind at Holger—the ropes were straining in their hands—at that moment he had noticed a cat lying limp on its side on the deck. It was dead. As if his mind no longer controlled what he was doing, he left his task and crouched down in front of it, a gray cat, a delicate frame under soaking wet fur. Carefully he picked it up and stood with it in his hands for a moment, held by some inner concentration, and carried it to the ship's side, whispered a word of offering, and dropped it into the sea. The cat bobbed on the swell and grew smaller as the ship continued its course, before being enveloped in a wave and vanishing from sight. Was it a sign, was the cat an omen that something was about to change? There was no one to interpret it. Holger had approached and stood with his eyes on Áslakr, who had gone silent and strange. How odd, he said. I wonder what it died of. Áslakr did not reply. Out of the blue like that, Holger went on, but when Áslakr responded only with a blunt, yes, so it seems, Holger returned to his work. Áslakr stood with his hands propped against the gunwale and looked out across the sea. What am I doing here? he asked himself. The ship, big and stable, made good headway through the water, across it, but although the wind filled the sail well, the journey home seemed suddenly all too long. Áslakr saw only cold and gray sky, cold and gray sea. Somewhere out there among the waves, the cat was spiraling down, further and further into the unknown, now it was smaller than nothing, he shuddered and wanted only to be ashore. He would hold Folkví's head to his abdomen and stroke her hair, and as the rain beat against his unfeeling skin, the months and the many experiences that had come between them lost their meaning: the Sæterland, the dream of another life, what had he been thinking? Separation is a gigantic betrayal. He had forgotten to think about her, and only now did he grasp that she'd had to look after herself every single day while he'd been away, how she must have struggled to keep herself strong. The time had surely been long and trying for her, he could not piece together how it must have gone, had no real sense of what made up her life when he wasn't there. The person she was then, and how she filled her days, muttering to herself no doubt, making offerings on his behalf to keep him safe. He drummed his fingers on the gunwale and was quite alone among the crew, the same way the ship was alone, surrounded on all sides by water. Surrounded by something alien to a man. When evening came he lay with his hands folded underneath his head, his eyes closed as he tried to recall his childhood home in detail: Just to the right of the door, what used to be there? But it only made him more distraught. All the time, he kept seeing her face with a look of what seemed to be expectancy, come on, she'd say, what then, what happens next? He saw how she would liven up when he came home. His back ached, he found no peace. He opened his eyes and stared up into a sparkling, starry black sky, concentrated on lying still, captive as he was in the self-contained world of the ship. A desire to shake the legs, to step away from where he was. During the course of that night he decided he wasn't going to drink anymore, stop indulging in the superficial bluster of the hird, intoxication wasn't the freedom he had thought it was. The acute sense of missing someone you very nearly let go seized him completely. His movements slowed, constrained by a mournfulness and foreboding that extended well into the following days, all the way up to their arrival at Ripa.

The Summer
of the Offering

Folkví has not slept. She has kept vigil all night in the offering shed. Has sat immersed in herself and seen very clearly what must happen. She opens the door of the house where behind the curtain Áslakr and Gerd lie sleeping, if sleeping is what they're doing. She dismisses the thought as soon as it visits her. A test has taken shape. It's the third day of the wedding, and the world must give a sign.

But she does not feel lightened. She blackens her eyes, wetting a finger and drawing it upward, smearing the paste into her skin. She seats herself on a bench among the sleeping guests. They are in the same house, she, ever the child, Áslakr and Gerd in the adults' domain. Something is out of step, and although the tree has sprouted up through her back to show the way, when she looks at

Áslakr she becomes small and weak, for she can sense that he continues to deny his trueborn sister. It has been like this all through the wedding: She has kept her distance, stealing looks at him. She notices the little ways he avoids her and speaks to others when they are in a group. It's as if he has forgotten the half of who he is, so she remembers for them both. The morning will determine if it can go on like this.

She puts on her blue cloak, closes the heavy lid of the chest, carefully, so none of the guests will wake. It'll be far too warm, yet this is how it must be, and it's barely dawn. Outside, the dew has fallen. She could probably drop an iron pot on the floor and not a grunt would come from the big men with their faces crumpled in sleep, nonetheless she takes care not to make a sound, tiptoeing through the long-room, heavy though her heart is. Like a child, she pulls back the curtain of the berth, inhales the odor of people and alcohol. Áslakr, her beautiful brother, lies there with an arm around his wife, so naturally, so incongruously, as if they were family. She wants to kiss him but cannot risk him waking, what would he say? All would be foiled. Instead she must focus on completing her task. That's where the decision lies, it is as she has taught herself: when once you begin, you must not hesitate, as happened all those times when she wasn't strong. This time will be different, no matter what.

Gerd stirs as Folkví grips her shoulder. She is even more luminous and slender in her night sark. She blinks her eyes and is about to say something, but Folkví hushes her. Come with me, she whispers, and all the bitterness of the previous days has left her, now she looks upon Gerd almost with indifference, it's no one's fault. It's the Norns and their stupid tapestry. Gerd looks around her, looks at Áslakr, but he's drunk and will not wake. Come on, Folkví whispers again, more insistent now, and takes her hand. The young woman unwinds herself cautiously from Áslakr's grasp before turning the covers aside and following Folkví across the floor. Put on a dress. Her voice trembles, but Gerd doesn't notice. Folkví is aquiver, she drinks from her flask and draws the curtain on Áslakr again while she waits. So, I'm doing this, a distant voice inside her says, and she sees herself performing these actions as if in a dream. As if she were outside herself, assessing her movements, they seem confident. The way her weight rests on one leg only, there's something relaxed about it. Her assured appearance invigorates her, she reacts to her own behavior, is buoyed up, this is something she can do well. With movements that are dazed and uncertain, Gerd finds herself a long dress, her eyes still puffy with sleep. She looks at Folkví, hesitant and uncomprehending. We're going to ensure the bloodline, come on. And Gerd puts on the dress, silent all the while. Folkví hands her a cup. Gerd is hesitant. There's something not right about there being just the two of them, normally there'd be a gathering. A moment later she reaches out and with both hands grips a table for support. Ah, she says, and her knees give way. Folkví studies her briefly. Come here, let me carry you.

She picks up Gerd's slight frame in its light-colored dress and carries her outside. Gerd's eyes open and close. She carries her across the silent yard and pushes open the door of the offering shed. The torches are alight inside, Gerd stirs, Folkví holds her tight, an arm around her neck. Their eyes meet, Gerd thinks Folkví is helping her. Then Folkví puts her down on the table and locks her head against her stomach, presses the cup to her lips. The liquid runs into Gerd's mouth. Folkví is the stronger of them. Soon Gerd's head flops to one side, she has drifted into a sleep that may last a very long time.

Outside the offering shed Folkví has a handcart ready,

she eases Gerd onto the bed, then takes off her blue cloak and covers her with it. There is an abundance of energy in her movements, she executes them awkwardly, but she is in the thick of it now. Perhaps even it is halfway done. She hauls away with the cart, following the line of the fence, out through the gate. She meets two thralls standing watch and nods at them. A sense of unreality thrums in her.

On her way down to the fjord she nearly forgets what she has resolved to do, struggling with the unwieldy cart feels almost like an end in itself. She pulls it along paths, dusty beams of sunlight falling through the trees in the dripping early dawn. There is a beauty in the scene that is all its own, the body laboring, the occasional glimpse of glittering water. The terrain is uneven. She wipes her brow and checks on Gerd, lying under the cloak on the little cart, and Folkví gasps on seeing how fine she is. A lovely, sleeping child. She smooths a finger lightly across her cheek, but what she sees is only a sheath. She covers her again and forges ahead.

As they near the fjord, the reality of the situation becomes apparent, now she is approaching the crux. What will the sign be? Folkví will know when she sees it, she tells herself. Then she will know. She comes to the top of a rise, and in the landscape before her the fjord lies open, above its waters the sky has drawn a protective arc of red. Like a rainbow entirely of red. That's it, she thinks, could it be any clearer? If that's not the sign, what is, and she trembles inside and out. It's permitted. She takes a swig from the flask at her belt, unsure whether to sit for a moment. She lifts the cloak and looks at Gerd. Now it's permitted, she says to her tender face. She wants to sit for a moment and take it all in, sense her body and let it go, comprehend the violence that lies ahead, but the situation feels too hectic. She looks around. There is no one to be seen, only the cows in the dale. And yet she can't shake the feeling that time is of the essence. The decision is made. She cannot linger, she must get it done.

It's hard to edge the cart down the slope without losing control of it, the gentle descent lends it momentum. She braces her back against it, trembling still, the handle digs into her flesh as she proceeds. The ground levels out and she quickens her pace, veering away to the fjord, following the path that hugs the shore, a rush of energy, she is breathless now, a fluster of nerves. Birds flap into the air, the light moves across the water. The red, red arc, and the offering site awaits. I must take note of every detail, she says to herself, but she cannot, everything flies past, there is a layer between her and the world. It's not as solemn as she expected, and before she knows it she is there. The offering site's little beech tree is almost red, everything is almost red in this strange light of the sky.

She rolls Gerd off the cart, carefully, so as not to injure her sedated body. Folkví looks up, into the arc, and tests Gerd, there at the foot of the tree. The sky must be her sign, but still she tests her. May I? she says, and takes another swig from her flask. A breath of wind passes through the treetops, a flutter of leaves, there. She places her hands on Gerd and chants a rhyme. Out of the clear day another breeze rustles through the tree, and she opens her eyes. She's beginning to feel dizzy. Should Gerd be tested one more time? But no, the answer is given. The wind in the tree, and the sky unlike anything she's ever seen. Today, everything exists for her benefit. She looks up into the leaves, but without her asking anything, the crown is virtually still.

She lifts the cloak from Gerd and as she throws it around herself Gerd begins to stir, her movements twisted as if to shield her face. There's some fight in her after all, pointless as it is. Folkví shakes the drowsy body until Gerd's head thuds against the ground and once more she is still. Humming, Folkví lies down and begins to drift, for the voice has its own will, it calls upon her mother's powers, and the demons of the forest. Gerd's body lies unmoving. She smooths her hands over herself and in a daze gulps from the flask one last time, lies down next to Gerd, and turns onto her side. They are face-to-face. She repeats her rhyme, in bright, clear tones.

At first only a ringing in her ears and an unavailing restlessness. Nothing happens. She tries to remain earnest, but maybe that plan was futile anyway, and immediately she wonders how she will explain it to Gerd when she wakes, this harsh treatment. She is angry with herself, a whole night in elevated communion with the spirits, not least the dream-tree that she took for a promise. To even have imagined the dead would help her. And she is about to sit up then in pure frustration, to have overestimated herself to such a degree. But all at once it kicks in with a surge, and she is hurled backward into darkness. The last thing she thinks is: it won't hurt to succumb awhile to such abrupt and overwhelming fatigue.

In the midst of the emptiness, a quivering sensation is followed by a searing pain in the bridge of her nose as

Gerd enters her body with her inhaled breath. Folkví's body draws her in. A specific point of pain as Gerd squeezes inside, then a pressure in her head and chest, there isn't room for two. And out she herself seeps, out through her sex and into the young woman's body beside her. Her entry by way of the nose is seamless, Gerd having already left the body. She registers how different the air feels on this unfamiliar skin, the sun against her back, a stone beneath her hip, before she is swallowed again by darkness.

When she comes to, her head hurts where it struck the ground, she is confused and nauseated. Blinking, she looks into the face that used to be hers. Her former body lies sleeping. What has she done? She wasn't even sure she had such powers. She sees her old face, how much she resembled Áslakr. A person never really knows their own features as well as those of their family. She senses the weight of her new body, or rather its lack of weight, how unusually light it is, quite differently distributed. She stretches out an arm and stares at the unfamiliar hand, the fingers, too short now. She feels like screaming. Her palm is too pink. Her new nose pokes strangely into her field of vision. She pushes the hair from the forehead of her old body, her eyes sting, but there's no time to fall into thought. Gerd must not wake. And it is done. Dazed, she gets to her feet.

Her old body was bigger-boned and stronger than the new, she struggles to haul it to the water's edge, must grip the armpits to drag it over the ground. Pebbles are disturbed. She looks away, and then, before she knows it, the long hair fans out into the fjord that mirrors the strange sky. She counts to ten, takes off her dress, and wades into the water, with all her might pulls her former body from the shore. It's hard not to cry, but the morning is beautiful. The body floats freely now, the blue cloak wafting like a mat, the loose hair. Almost without thinking, she does what she must, presses the body down into the water, a hand on its chest, and some bubbles rise. She sees the face below the surface. The reflection of her new face angled beside it. But mostly she sees the face of her kin, young, strong-featured, a covering of water, and then the face opens its eyes. They are clear and gray. For a long moment the two women stare at each other, the body in the water begins to struggle, arms and legs thrash, the submerged face opens its mouth in a scream, but Folkví is on top, pressing it under, until the bubbles of air cease. She lets the body float out into the still water, follows it awhile, guiding it away from the offering site, the water gets deeper, it reaches to her chest, and all at once she vomits, then, erratically, half swimming, half wading, propels herself toward shore. Gasping sobs escape from her throat, she gazes at the slick surface of the fjord, the beautiful body, the person she was, while putting her dress back on. The treetops whisper above her head, there's a smell of soil and sorrel. She pulls the cart into some bushes and dries herself with her dress.

From the top of the rise she looks back one last time at the fjord. Gerd has drifted away and is very small now, Folkví raises a hand in farewell. The red sky has dissolved, it's as if she's waking from a nightmare. The worst of all outcomes, but I couldn't bear to lose you. There is no strength in her arms and legs, yet she carries on walking. No, she cries out. Folkví empties her lungs, it's insurmountable. What a person will do for love, what they will do to feel secure. She clutches a tree for support.

Outside the headman's yard she collects herself. Her skin is dry again, she puts up her hair so its damp ends will not be seen. Her dress is a little soiled. She must carry herself naturally and with dignity. She breathes in and feels a racing pulse thump in her body as she goes through the gate and nods at the two thralls. In front of the head-man's hall she sees Áslakr sitting with his back toward her among a group of men, and everything falls into place before her eyes, there he sits, her beloved, she walks briskly, following the fence at a trot almost, and enters their house. The curtain of their parents' berth has been drawn back. Now the bed is theirs. A new body, her old life. For a brief moment, she thinks she might lie down on her back, attend to her exhaustion, allow the morning to sink in, but Áslakr is just outside, that overshadows everything. They have no time to waste. She puts on a clean dress and pinches her cheeks, smiles at the people she meets as she crosses the yard in the direction of the group. She puts a finger in front of her lips so that the others will not give her away and steps up to Áslakr from behind. She throws her arms around him, the smell of his hair and skin fills her nostrils. He turns toward her and looks up. Gerd, so there you are, he says, and beams.

Acknowledgments

Thank you to everyone who read, discussed, and took an interest in the novel during the writing process. Thanks to my Danish publisher, Gutkind, and to Louise Kønigsfeldt, my editor there, for guidance and for believing in the project from an early stage.

Thanks also to Martin Aitken for his attentive translation, and to Riverhead and to Becky Saletan for her thoughtful editing. It's been a true pleasure working with you.

—*Maria Hesselager*

Thanks to Maria Hesselager and Becky Saletan for inspired and sensitive work in shaping the English text.

—*Martin Aitken*